nickelodeon

BREADWINNERS™

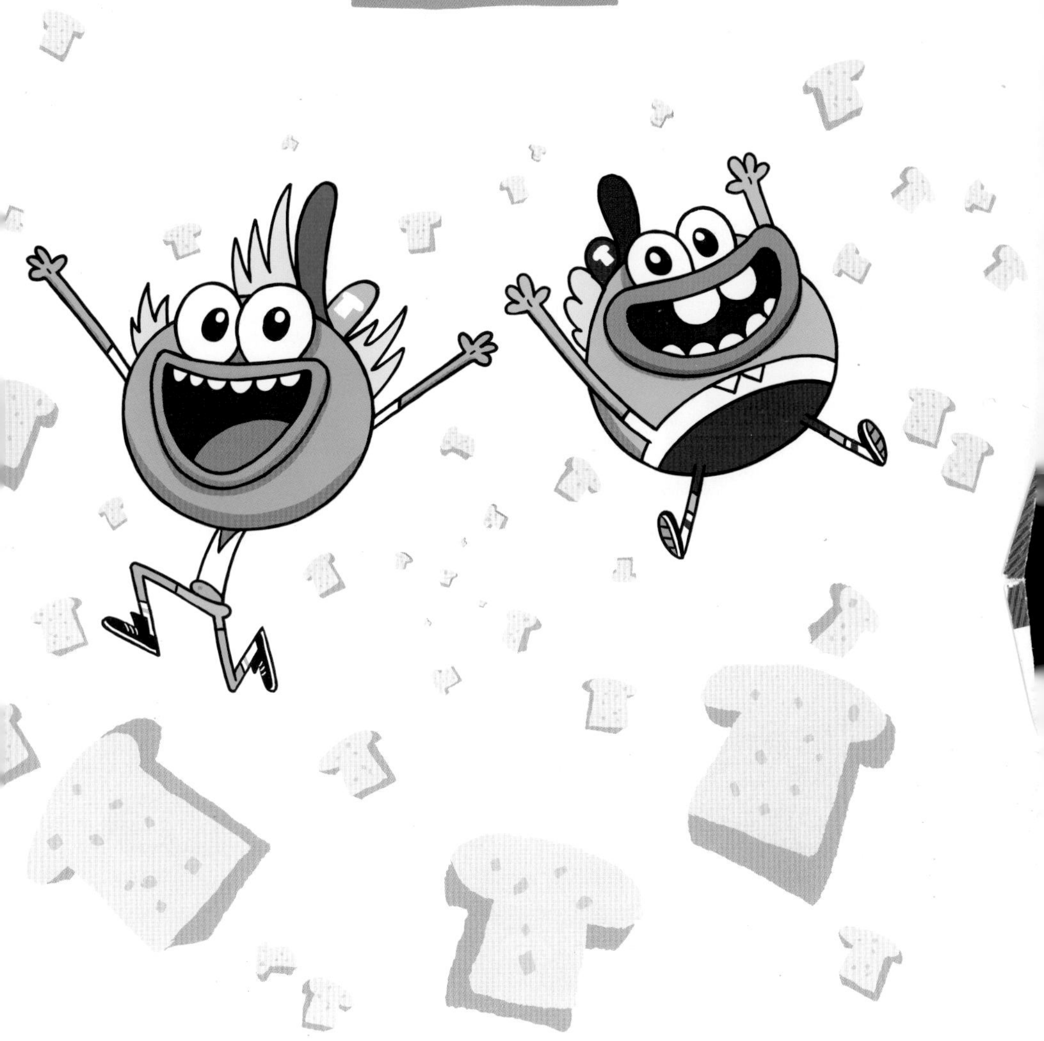

PAPERCUTZ™
New York

nickelodeon GRAPHIC NOVELS AVAILABLE FROM PAPERCUTZ

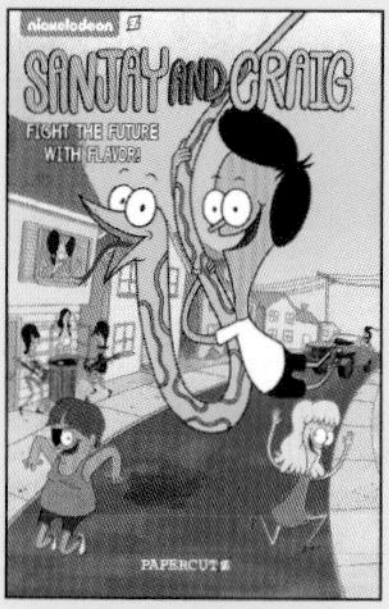
nickelodeon
SANJAY AND CRAIG
FIGHT THE FUTURE WITH FLAVOR
PAPERCUTZ

#1 "Fight the Future with Flavor"

COMING SOON!

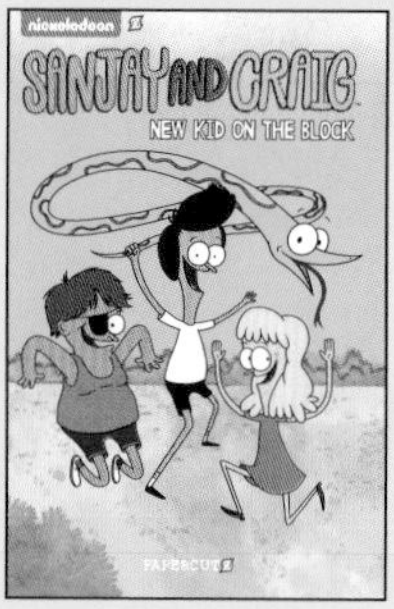
nickelodeon
SANJAY AND CRAIG
NEW KID ON THE BLOCK
PAPERCUTZ

#2 "New Kid on the Block"

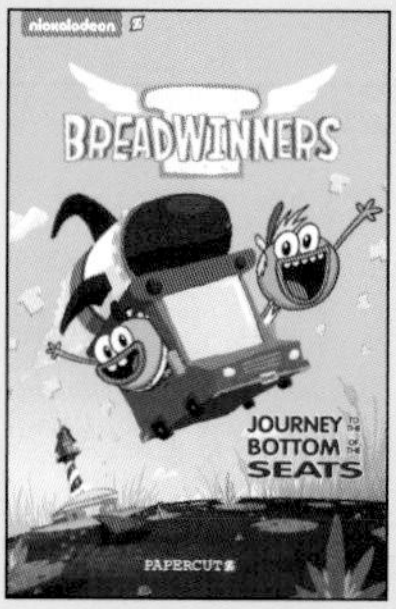
nickelodeon
BREADWINNERS
JOURNEY TO THE BOTTOM OF THE SEATS
PAPERCUTZ

#1 "Journey to the Bottom of the Seats"

COMING SOON!

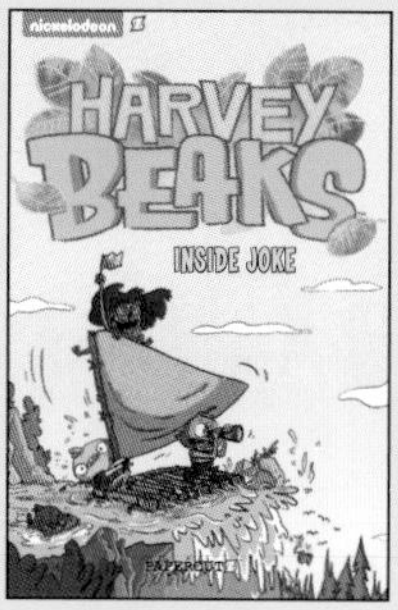
nickelodeon
HARVEY BEAKS
INSIDE JOKE
PAPERCUTZ

#1 "Inside Joke"

COMING SOO

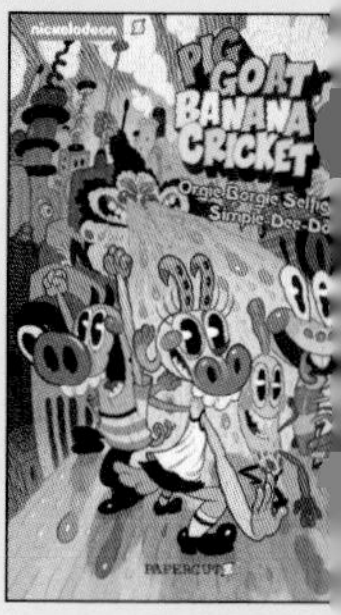
nickelodeon
PIG GOAT BANANA CRICKET
PAPERCUTZ

#1 "Orgle Borgle Se Simple-Dee-Doo!"

Nickelodeon graphic novels are available for $7.99 in paperback, $12.99 in hardcover. Available from booksellers everywhere. You can also order online from Papercutz.com. Or call 1-800-886-1223, Monday through Friday, 9-5 EST. MC, Visa, and AmEx accepted. To order by mail, please add $4.00 for postage and handling for first book ordered, $1.00 for each additional book and make check payable to NBM Publishing.
Send to: Papercutz, 160 Broadway, Suite 700, East Wing, New York, NY 10039.

Nickelodeon graphic novels are also available digitally wherever e-books are sold.

SUBSCRIBE!

The Greatest Kids Magazine in the world is here and you can be a charter subscriber. Be the first to get your copies and make sure you don't miss a single issue of the all-new Nickelodeon Magazine!

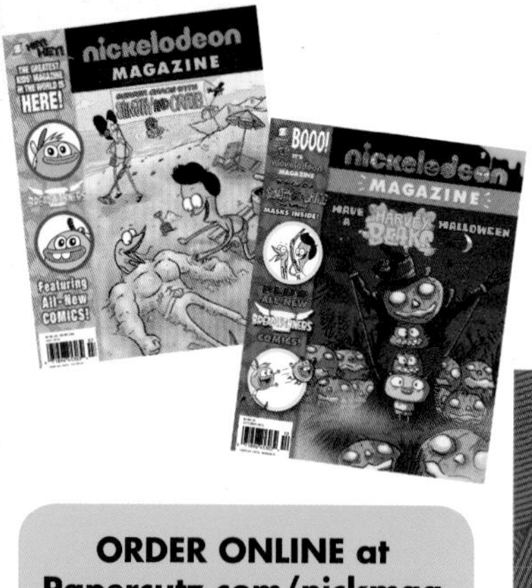
nickelodeon MAGAZINE
HERE!
Featuring All-New COMICS!
BOOO!
nickelodeon MAGAZINE
HARVEY BEAKS
HALLOWEEN
COMICS

Never miss an issue of

nickelodeon

MAGAZINE

Get Your Copies Delivered Right to Your Mailbox at Hom

ORDER ONLINE at Papercutz.com/nickmag

OR CALL 1-800-778-6278

(Please have debit/credit card ready)

Use promo code: BWGN1.

Save! And Get Free Issues

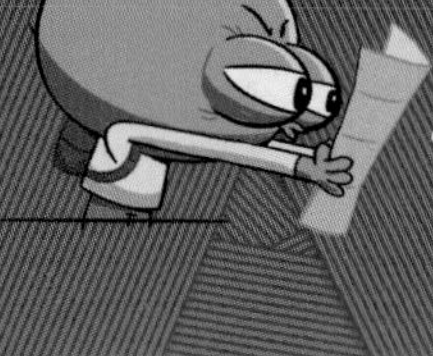

7 ISSUES FOR THE PRICE OF 6!

+SAVE $7 OFF COVER PRICE!

6 REGULAR ISSUES
+1 BONUS FREE ISSUE
7 ISSUES FOR ONLY $27

14 ISSUES FOR THE PRICE OF 12!

+SAVE $14 OFF COVER PRICE!

12 REGULAR ISSUES
+2 BONUS FREE ISSUE
14 ISSUES FOR ONLY $49.9

DIGITAL SUBSCRIPTION - ONLY $19.99 - OR FREE FOR ALL PRINT SUBS

nickelodeon

BREADWINNERS

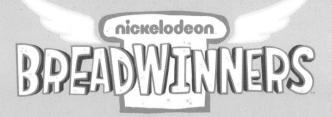

TABLE OF CONTENTS

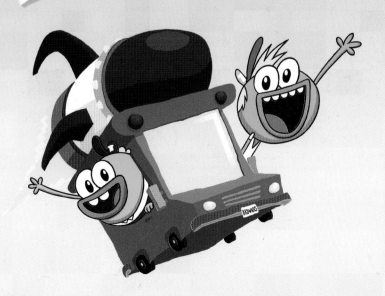

nickelodeon

BREADWINNERS

JOURNEY to the Bottom of the Seats

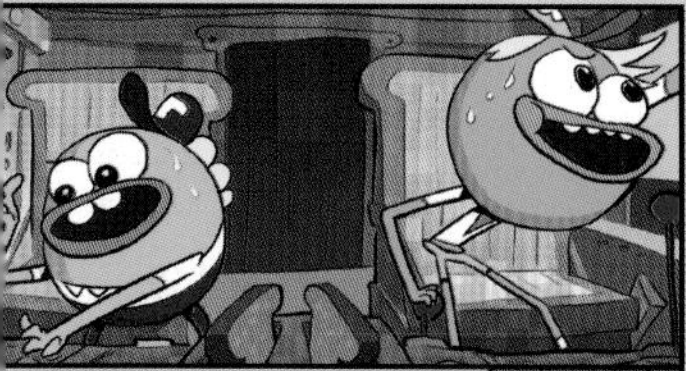

"LOTSA TOTS"
Stefan Petrucha – Writer
Allison Strejlau – Artist
Laurie E. Smith – Colorist
Tom Orzechowski – Letterer

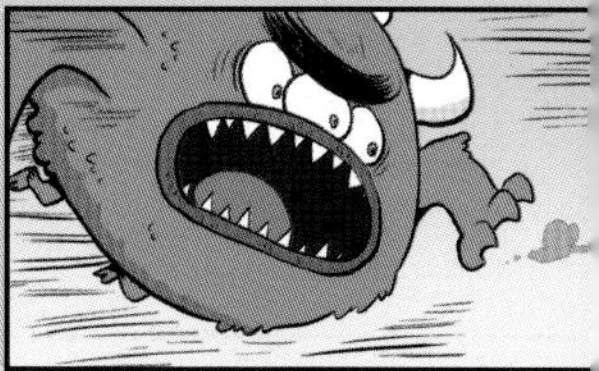

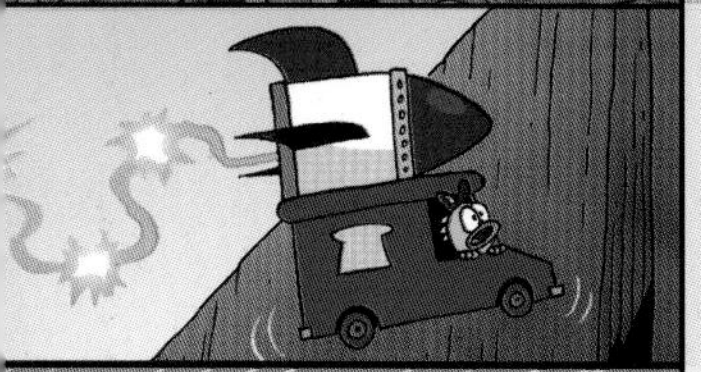

"JOURNEY TO THE BOTTOM OF THE SEATS"
Stefan Petrucha – Writer
Mike Kazaleh – Artist
Laurie E. Smith – Colorist
Tom Orzechowski – Letterer

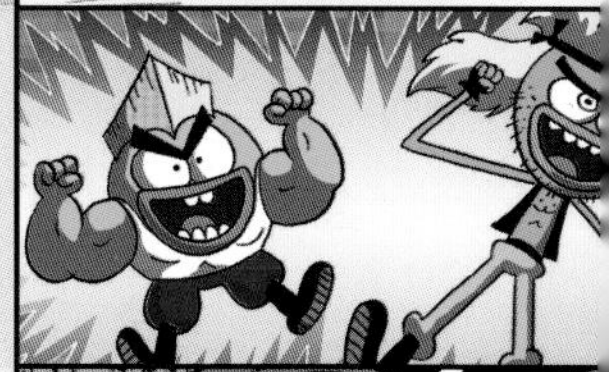

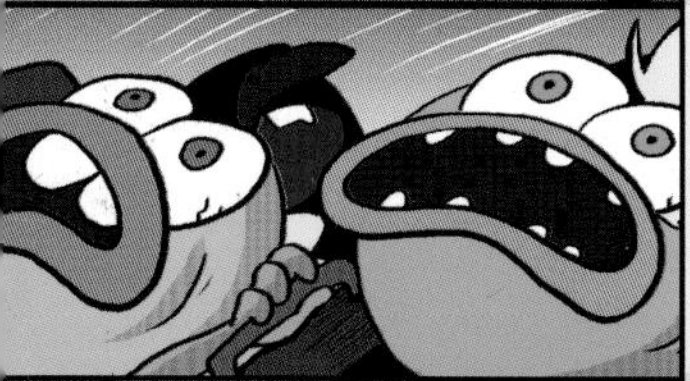

"CLOWN DOWN"
Stefan Petrucha – Writer
Allison Strejlau – Artist
Laurie E. Smith – Colorist
Tom Orzechowski – Letterer

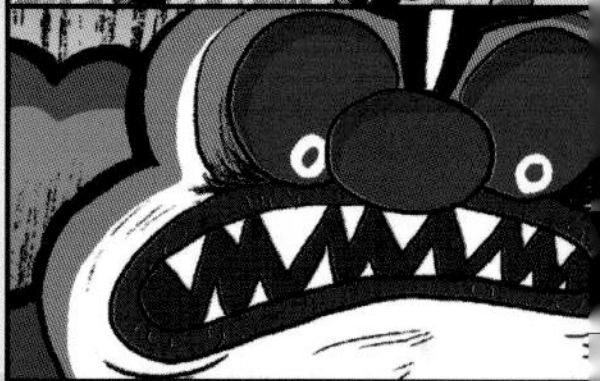

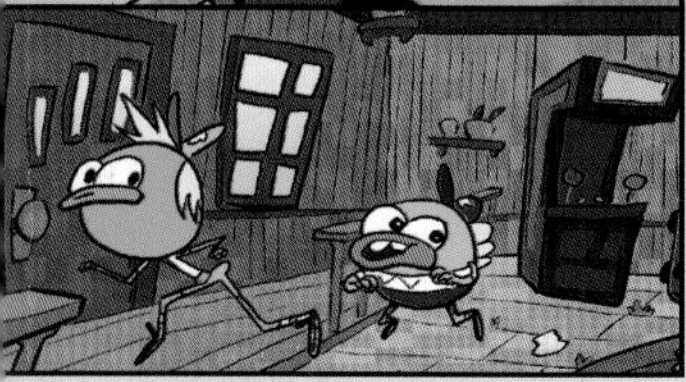

"MISSION SUSPICION"
Stefan Petrucha – Writer
Allison Strejlau – Artist
Laurie E. Smith – Colorist
Tom Orzechowski – Letterer

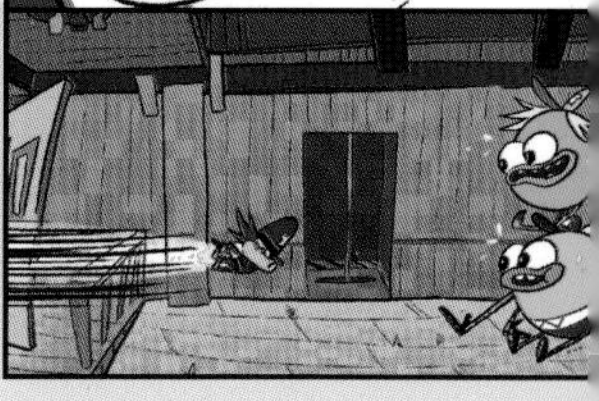

Based on the Nickelodeon animated
TV series created by
Gary "Doodles" DiRaffeale and Steve Borst.

Chris Nelson – Design/Production
James Salerno – Sr. Art Director/Nickelodeon
Jeff Whitman – Production Coordinator
Bethany Bryan, Suzannah Rowntree, Michael Petranek – Editors
Joan Hilty – Comics Editor/Nickelodeon
Dan Berlin, Dani Breckenridge – Editorial Interns
Jim Salicrup
Editor-in-Chief

ISBN: 978-1-62991-300-1 paperback edition
ISBN: 978-1-62991-301-8 hardcover edition

Printed in the USA through
Four Colour Print Group
November 2015 by Lifetouch Printing
5126 Forest Hills Ct., Loves Park, IL 61111

Distributed by Macmillan
First Printing

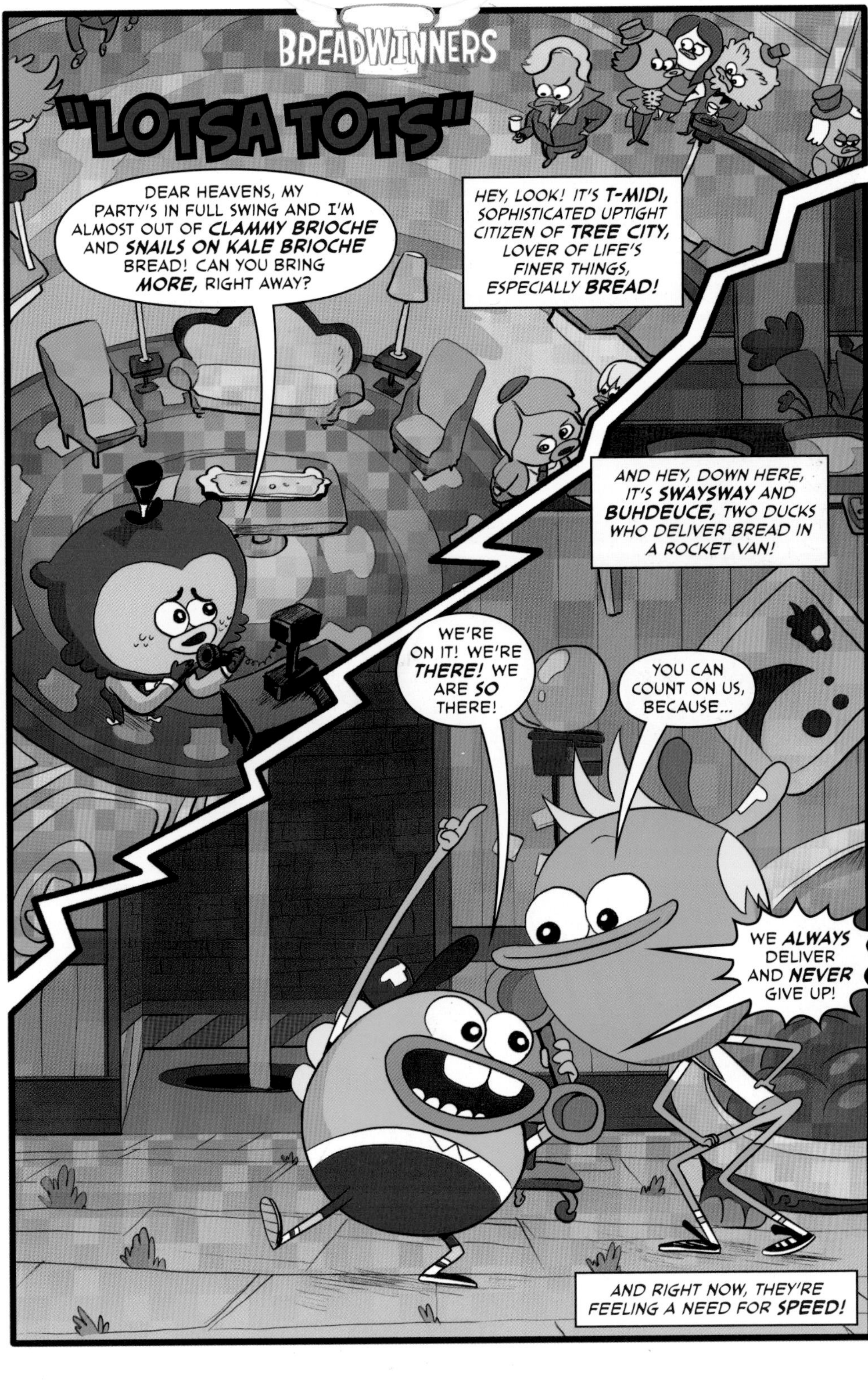
BREADWINNERS
"LOTSA TOTS"
DEAR HEAVENS, MY PARTY'S IN FULL SWING AND I'M ALMOST OUT OF CLAMMY BRIOCHE AND SNAILS ON KALE BRIOCHE BREAD! CAN YOU BRING MORE, RIGHT AWAY?
HEY, LOOK! IT'S T-MIDI, SOPHISTICATED UPTIGHT CITIZEN OF TREE CITY, LOVER OF LIFE'S FINER THINGS, ESPECIALLY BREAD!
AND HEY, DOWN HERE, IT'S SWAYSWAY AND BUHDEUCE, TWO DUCKS WHO DELIVER BREAD IN A ROCKET VAN!
WE'RE ON IT! WE'RE THERE! WE ARE SO THERE!
YOU CAN COUNT ON US, BECAUSE...
WE ALWAYS DELIVER AND NEVER GIVE UP!
AND RIGHT NOW, THEY'RE FEELING A NEED FOR SPEED!

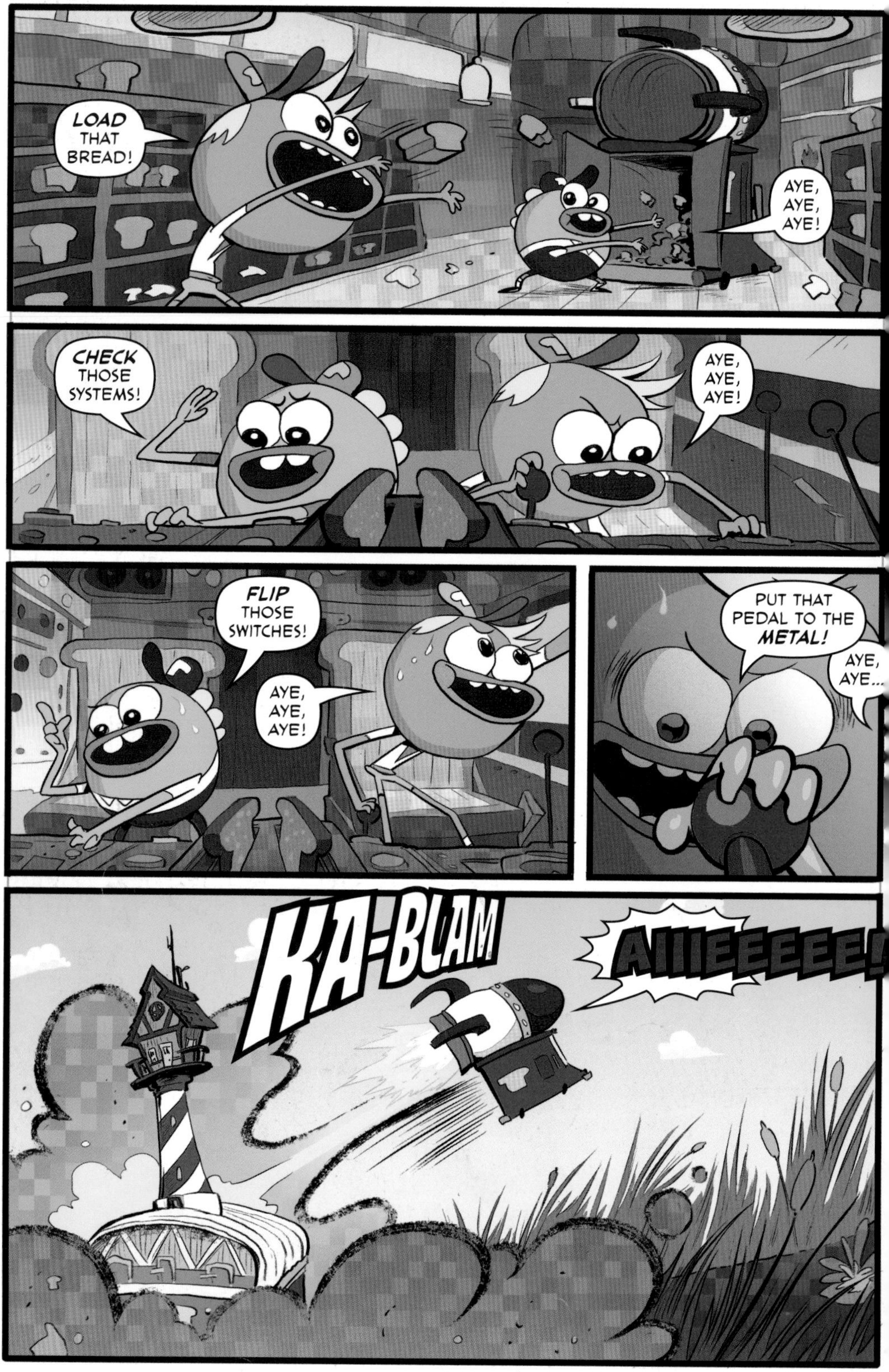
LOAD THAT BREAD!
AYE, AYE, AYE!
CHECK THOSE SYSTEMS!
AYE, AYE, AYE!
FLIP THOSE SWITCHES!
AYE, AYE, AYE!
PUT THAT PEDAL TO THE METAL!
AYE, AYE...
KA-BLAM
AIIIEEEEE!

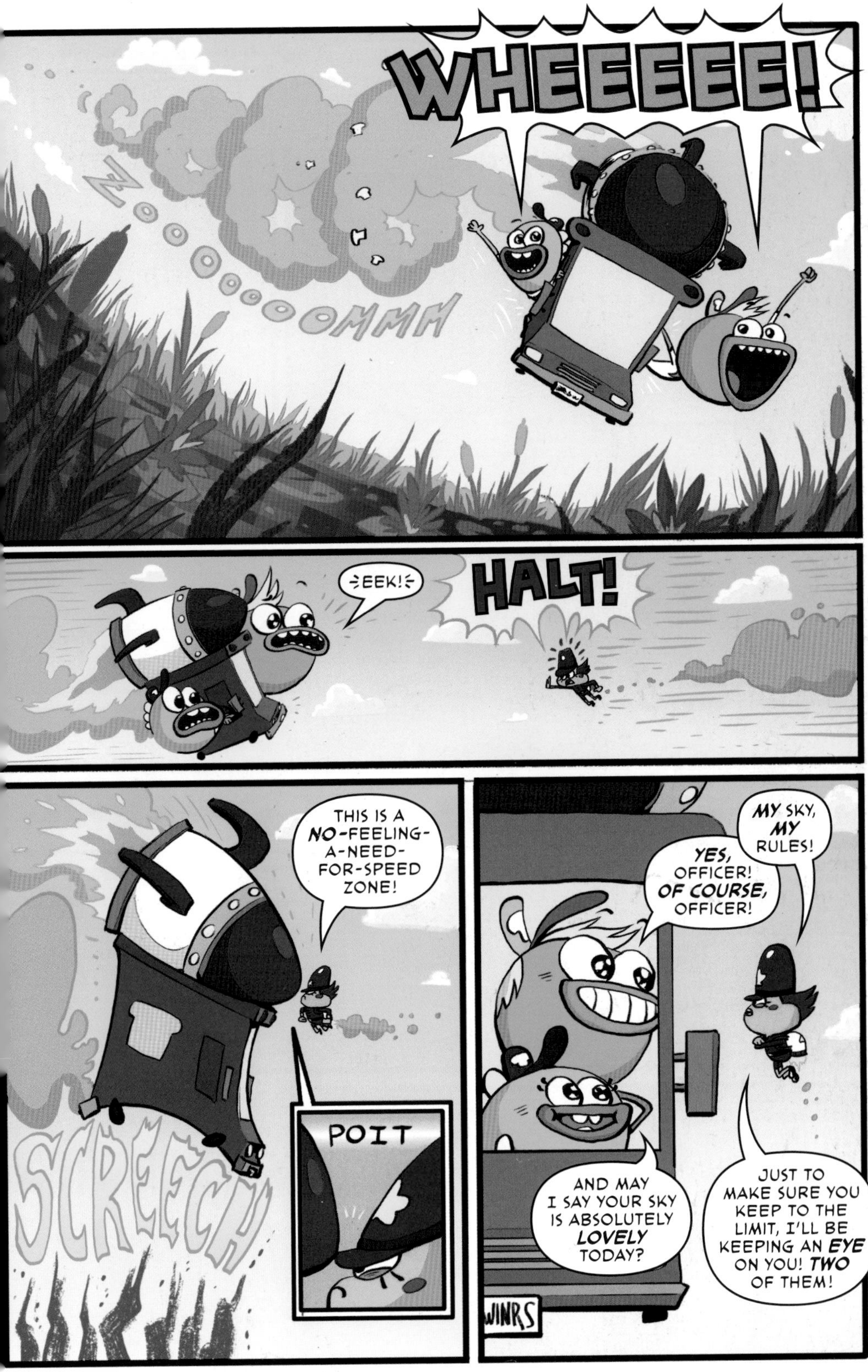
WHEEEEEE!
ZOOOoooOOMMM
EEK!
HALT!
THIS IS A NO-FEELING-A-NEED-FOR-SPEED ZONE!
POIT
SCREECH
YES, OFFICER! OF COURSE, OFFICER!
MY SKY, MY RULES!
WINRS
AND MAY I SAY YOUR SKY IS ABSOLUTELY LOVELY TODAY?
JUST TO MAKE SURE YOU KEEP TO THE LIMIT, I'LL BE KEEPING AN EYE ON YOU! TWO OF THEM!

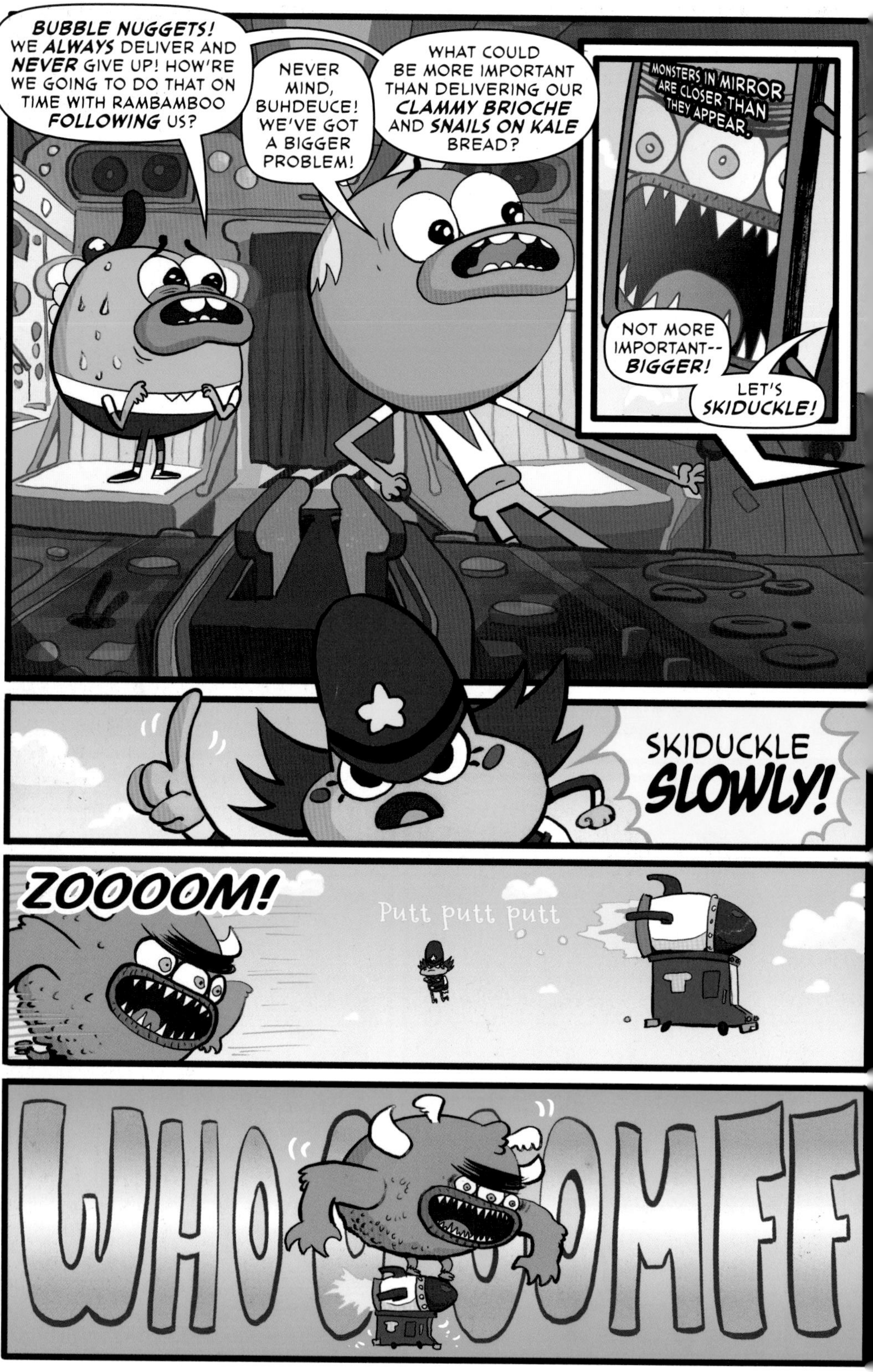

BUBBLE NUGGETS! WE ALWAYS DELIVER AND NEVER GIVE UP! HOW'RE WE GOING TO DO THAT ON TIME WITH RAMBAMBOO FOLLOWING US?
NEVER MIND, BUHDEUCE! WE'VE GOT A BIGGER PROBLEM!
WHAT COULD BE MORE IMPORTANT THAN DELIVERING OUR CLAMMY BRIOCHE AND SNAILS ON KALE BREAD?
MONSTERS IN MIRROR ARE CLOSER THAN THEY APPEAR.
NOT MORE IMPORTANT-- BIGGER!
LET'S SKIDUCKLE!
SKIDUCKLE SLOWLY!
ZOOOOM!
Putt putt putt
WHOOOOMFF

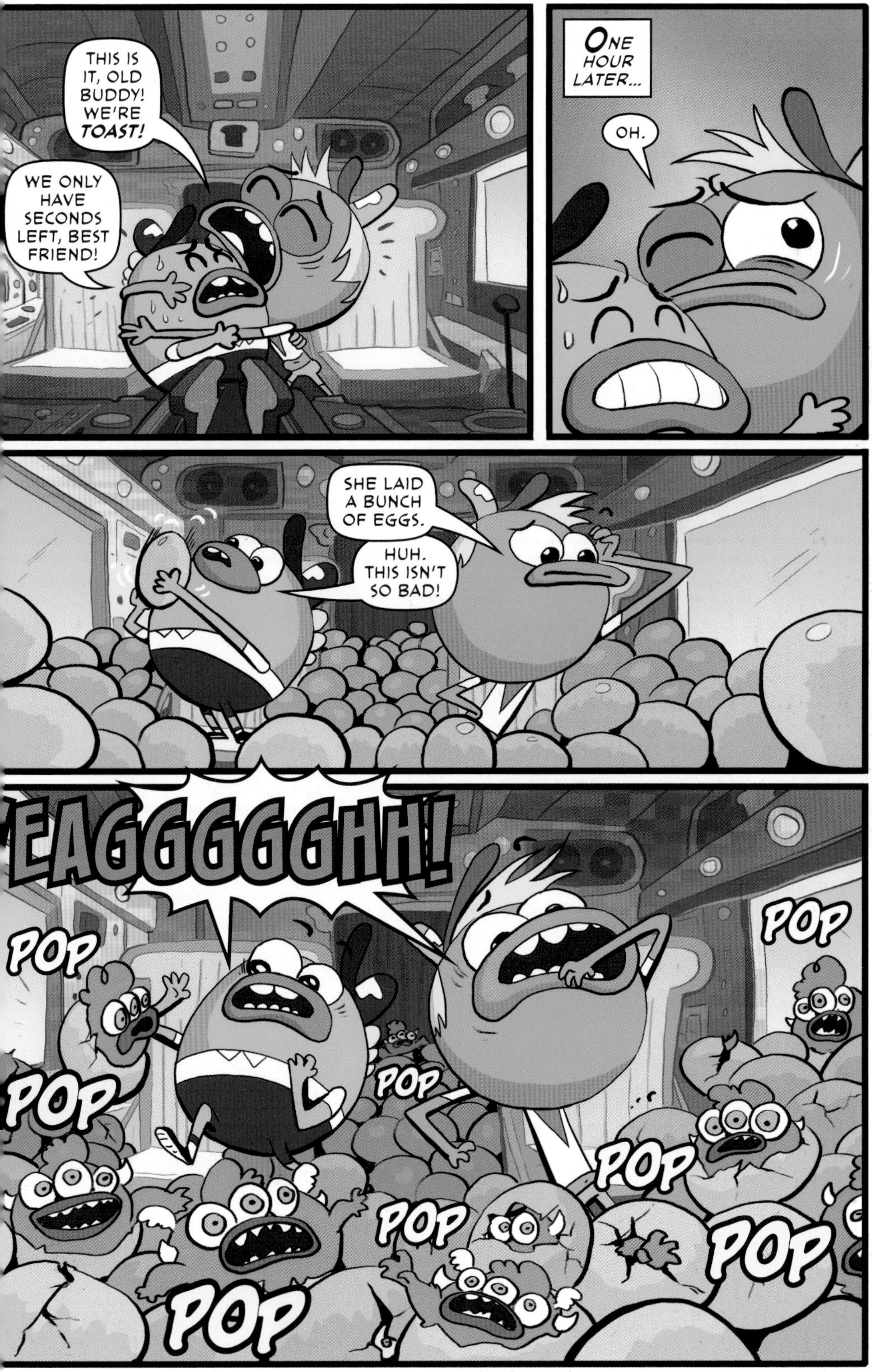
THIS IS IT, OLD BUDDY! WE'RE *TOAST!*
WE ONLY HAVE SECONDS LEFT, BEST FRIEND!
ONE HOUR LATER...
OH.
SHE LAID A BUNCH OF EGGS.
HUH. THIS ISN'T SO BAD!
EAGGGGGHH!
POP
POP
POP
POP
POP
POP
POP
POP

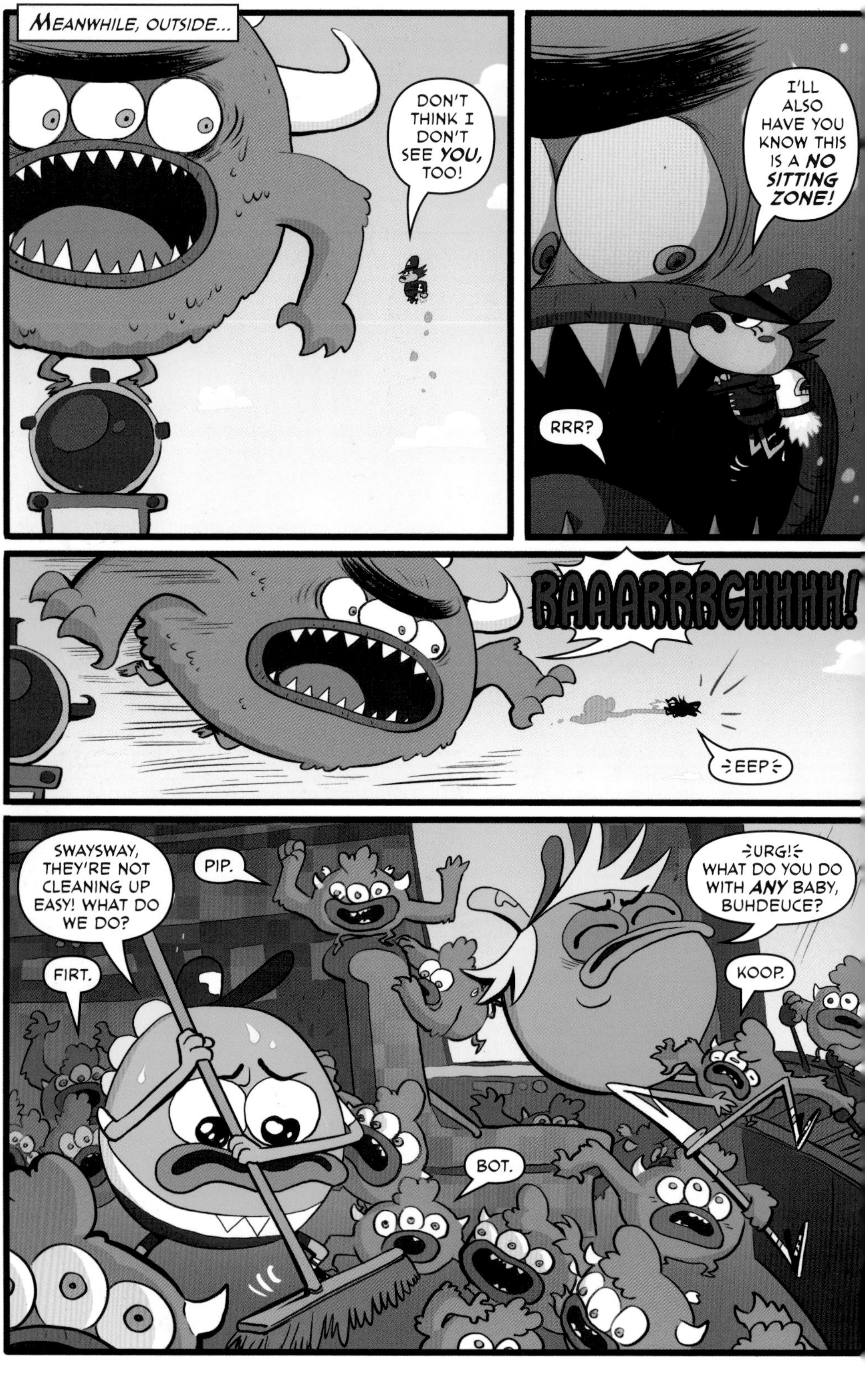
MEANWHILE, OUTSIDE...
DON'T THINK I DON'T SEE YOU, TOO!
I'LL ALSO HAVE YOU KNOW THIS IS A NO SITTING ZONE!
RRR?
RAAARRRGHHHH!
EEP
SWAYSWAY, THEY'RE NOT CLEANING UP EASY! WHAT DO WE DO?
PIP.
URG! WHAT DO YOU DO WITH ANY BABY, BUHDEUCE?
FIRT.
KOOP.
BOT.

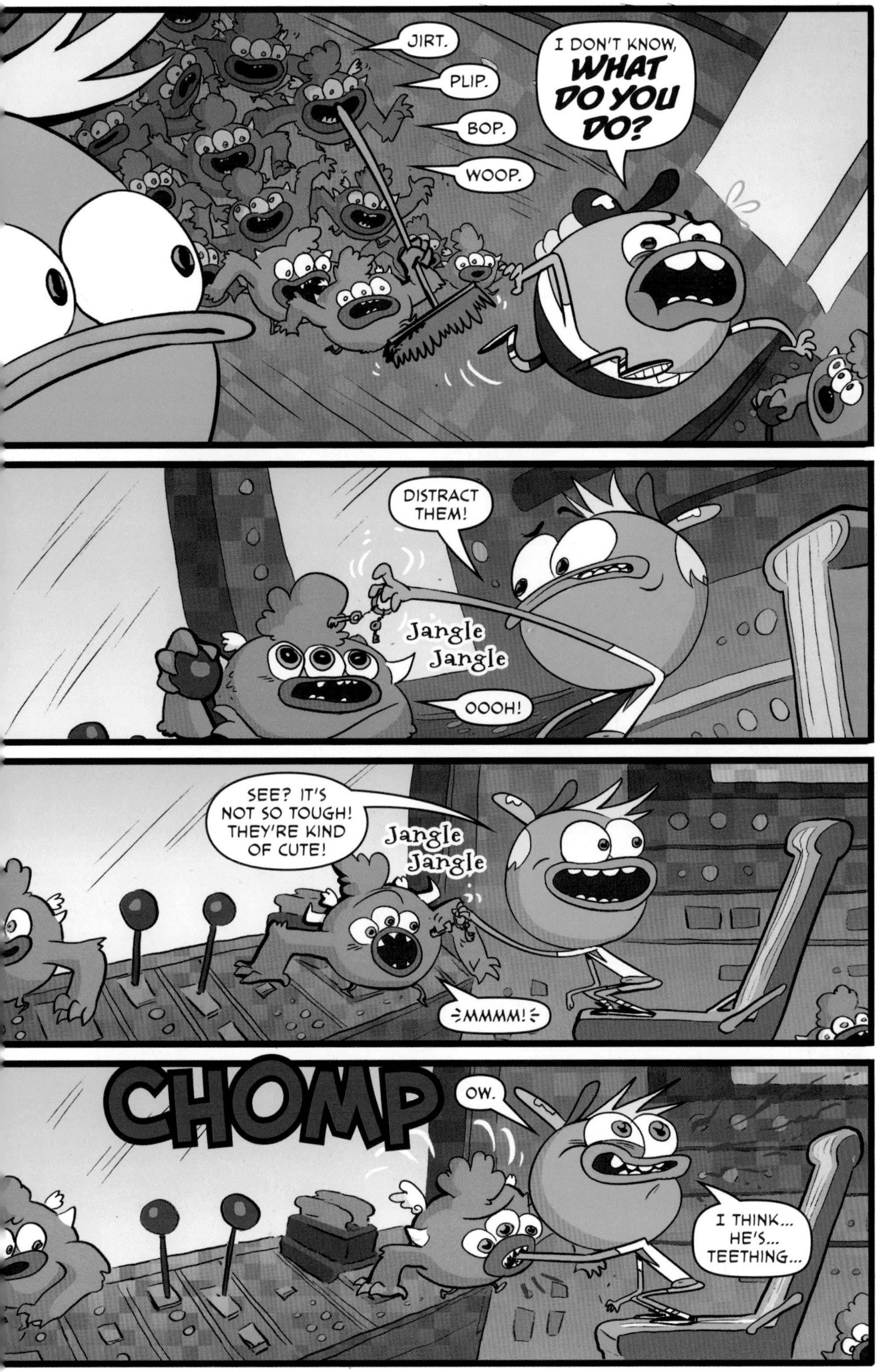
JIRT.
PLIP.
BOP.
WOOP.
I DON'T KNOW, WHAT DO YOU DO?
DISTRACT THEM!
Jangle Jangle
OOOH!
SEE? IT'S NOT SO TOUGH! THEY'RE KIND OF CUTE!
Jangle Jangle
MMMM!
CHOMP
OW.
I THINK... HE'S... TEETHING...

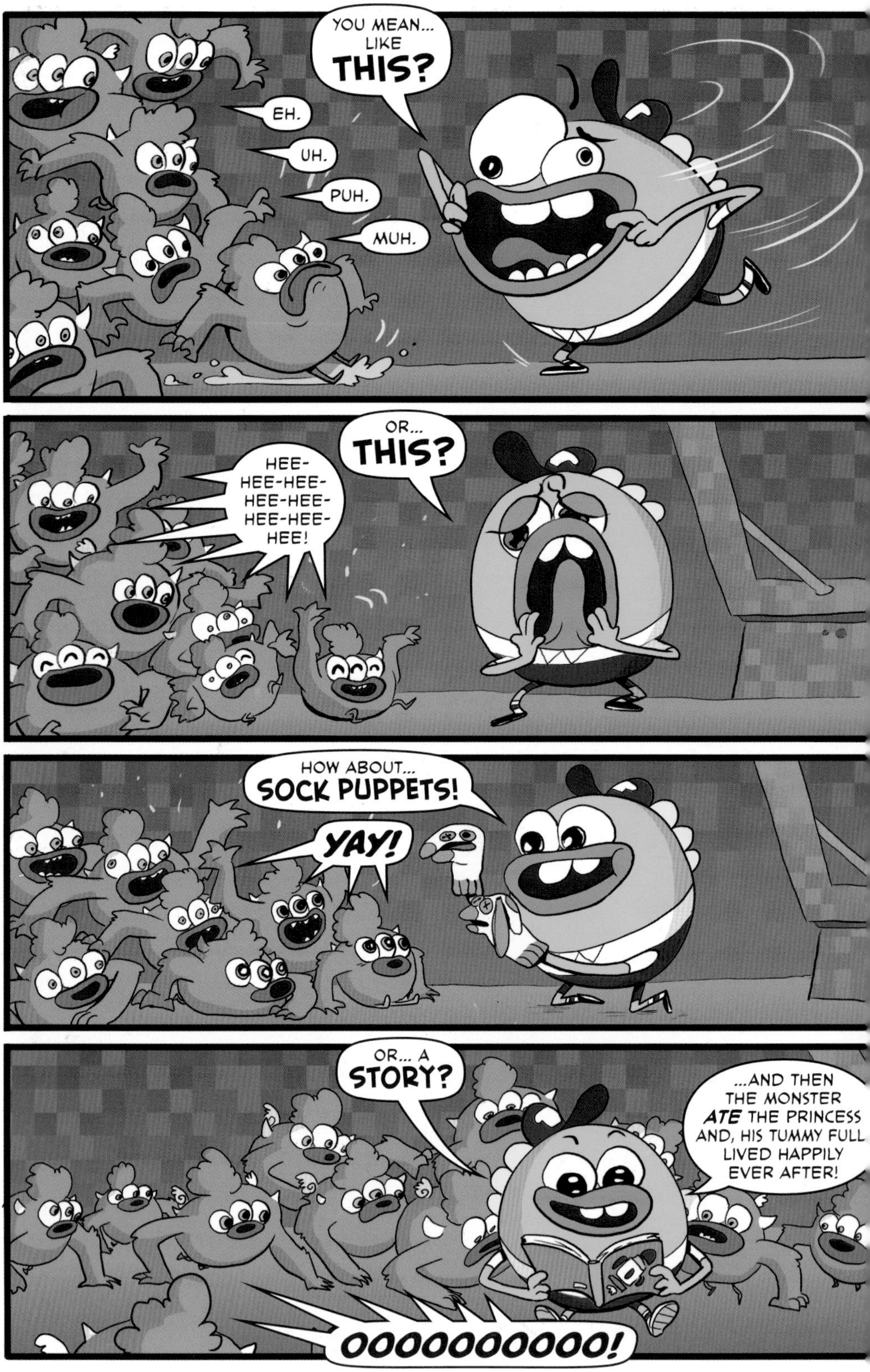
YOU MEAN... LIKE THIS?
EH.
UH.
PUH.
MUH.
OR... THIS?
HEE-HEE-HEE-HEE-HEE-HEE-HEE-HEE!
HOW ABOUT... SOCK PUPPETS!
YAY!
OR... A STORY?
...AND THEN THE MONSTER ATE THE PRINCESS AND, HIS TUMMY FULL LIVED HAPPILY EVER AFTER!
OOOOOOOOOO!

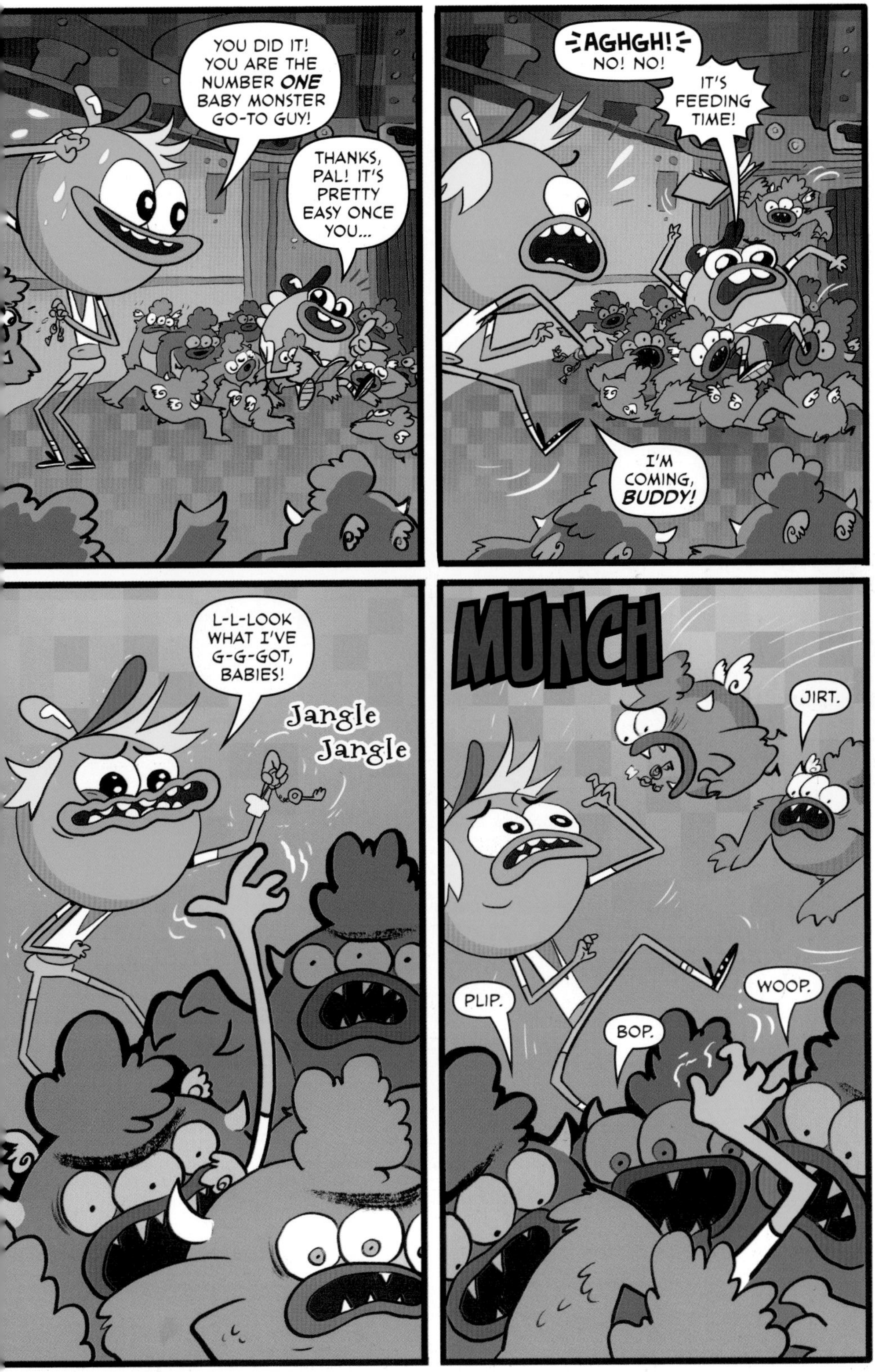
YOU DID IT! YOU ARE THE NUMBER ONE BABY MONSTER GO-TO GUY!
THANKS, PAL! IT'S PRETTY EASY ONCE YOU...
AGHGH! NO! NO!
IT'S FEEDING TIME!
I'M COMING, BUDDY!
L-L-LOOK WHAT I'VE G-G-GOT, BABIES!
Jangle Jangle
MUNCH
JIRT.
PLIP.
BOP.
WOOP.

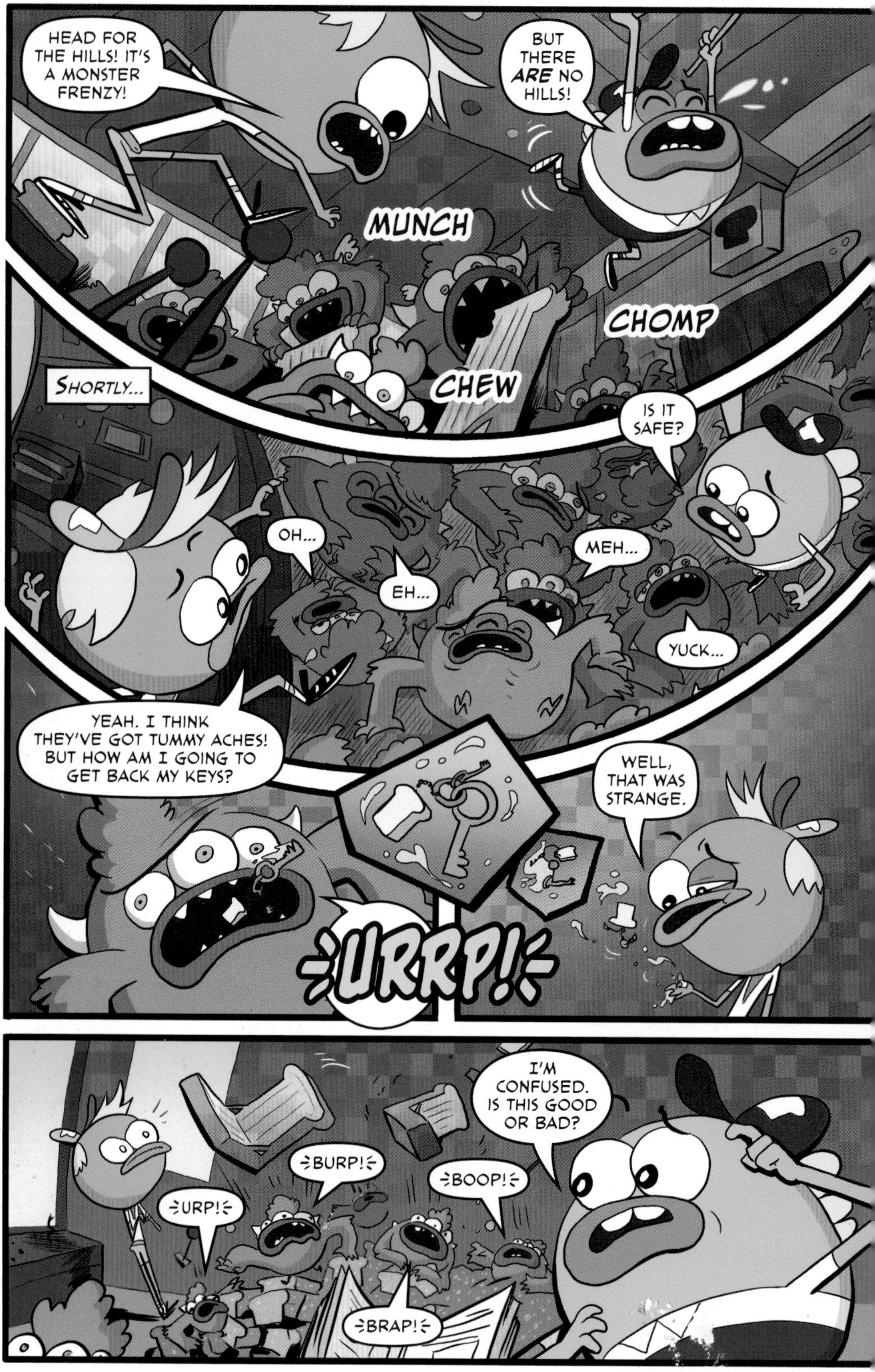

HEAD FOR THE HILLS! IT'S A MONSTER FRENZY!
BUT THERE ARE NO HILLS!
MUNCH
CHOMP
CHEW
SHORTLY...
IS IT SAFE?
OH...
EH...
MEH...
YUCK...
YEAH. I THINK THEY'VE GOT TUMMY ACHES! BUT HOW AM I GOING TO GET BACK MY KEYS?
WELL, THAT WAS STRANGE.
URRP!
I'M CONFUSED. IS THIS GOOD OR BAD?
BURP!
BOOP!
URP!
BRAP!

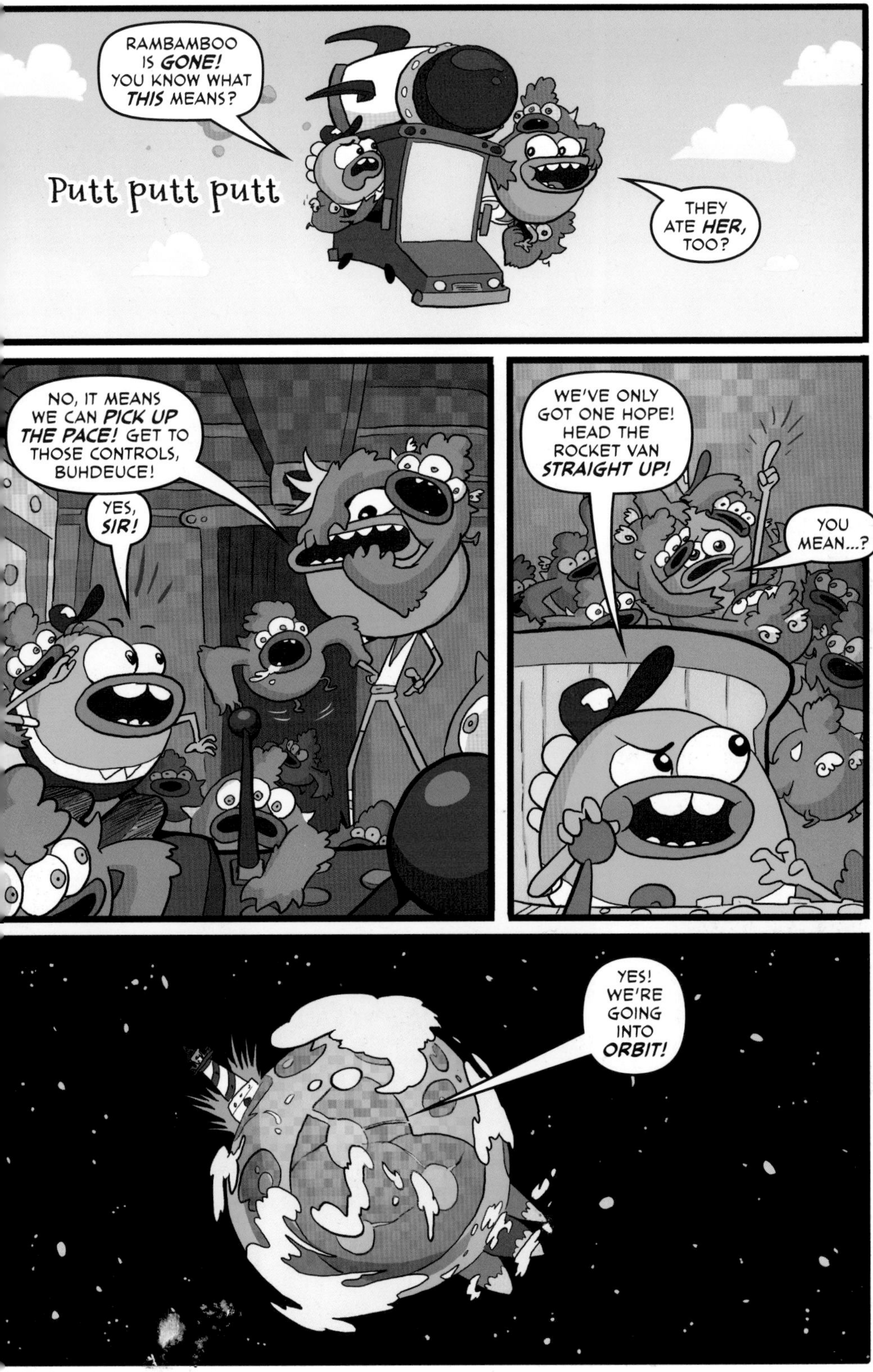

RAMBAMBOO IS GONE! YOU KNOW WHAT THIS MEANS?
Putt putt putt
THEY ATE HER, TOO?
NO, IT MEANS WE CAN PICK UP THE PACE! GET TO THOSE CONTROLS, BUHDEUCE!
YES, SIR!
WE'VE ONLY GOT ONE HOPE! HEAD THE ROCKET VAN STRAIGHT UP!
YOU MEAN...?
YES! WE'RE GOING INTO ORBIT!

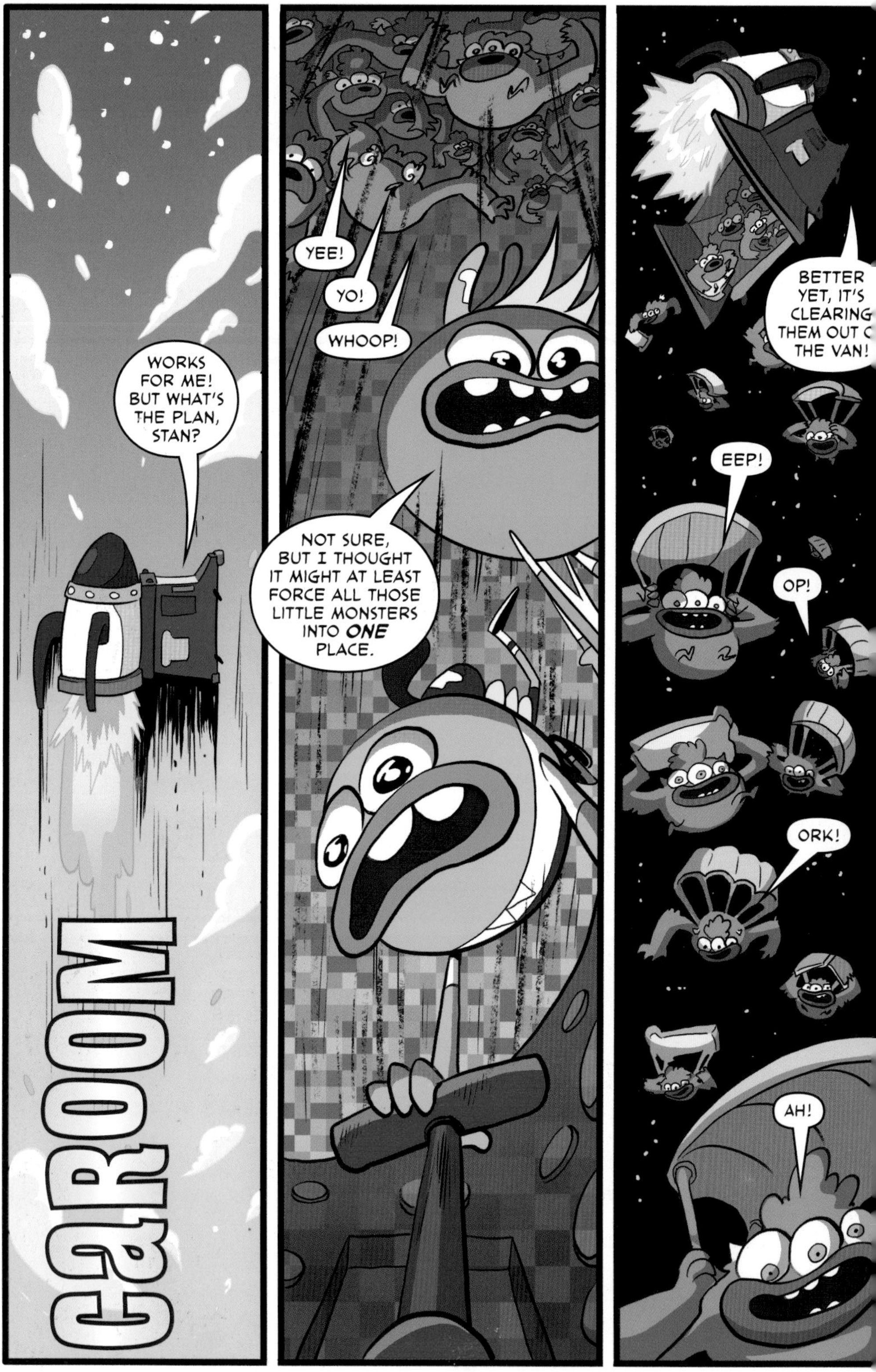
WORKS FOR ME! BUT WHAT'S THE PLAN, STAN?
CAROOOM
YEE!
YO!
WHOOP!
NOT SURE, BUT I THOUGHT IT MIGHT AT LEAST FORCE ALL THOSE LITTLE MONSTERS INTO *ONE* PLACE.
BETTER YET, IT'S CLEARING THEM OUT O THE VAN!
EEP!
OP!
ORK!
AH!

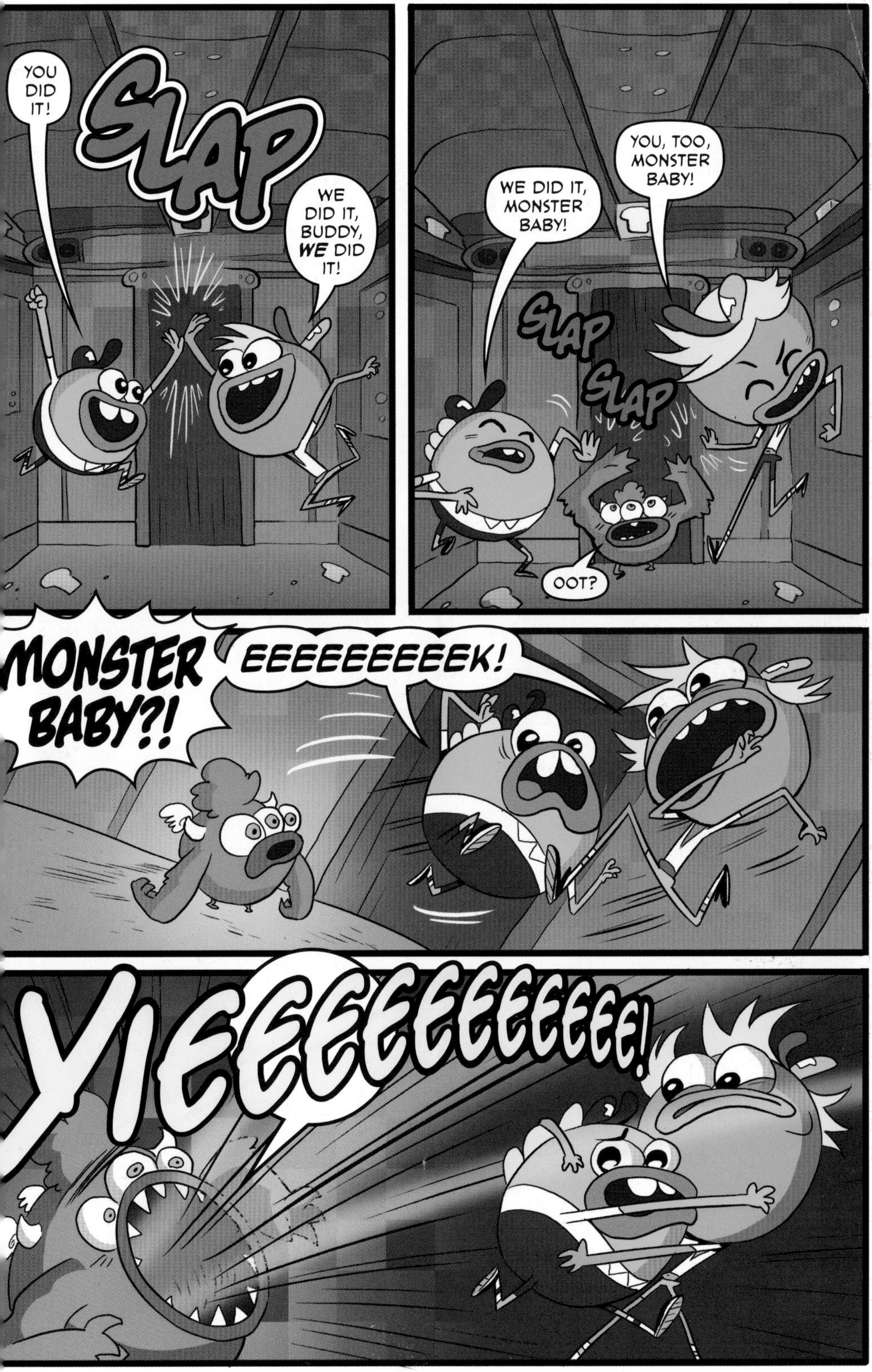
YOU DID IT!
SLAP
WE DID IT, BUDDY, WE DID IT!
YOU, TOO, MONSTER BABY!
WE DID IT, MONSTER BABY!
SLAP
SLAP
OOT?
MONSTER BABY?!
EEEEEEEEEEK!
YIEEEEEEEEEEEEE!

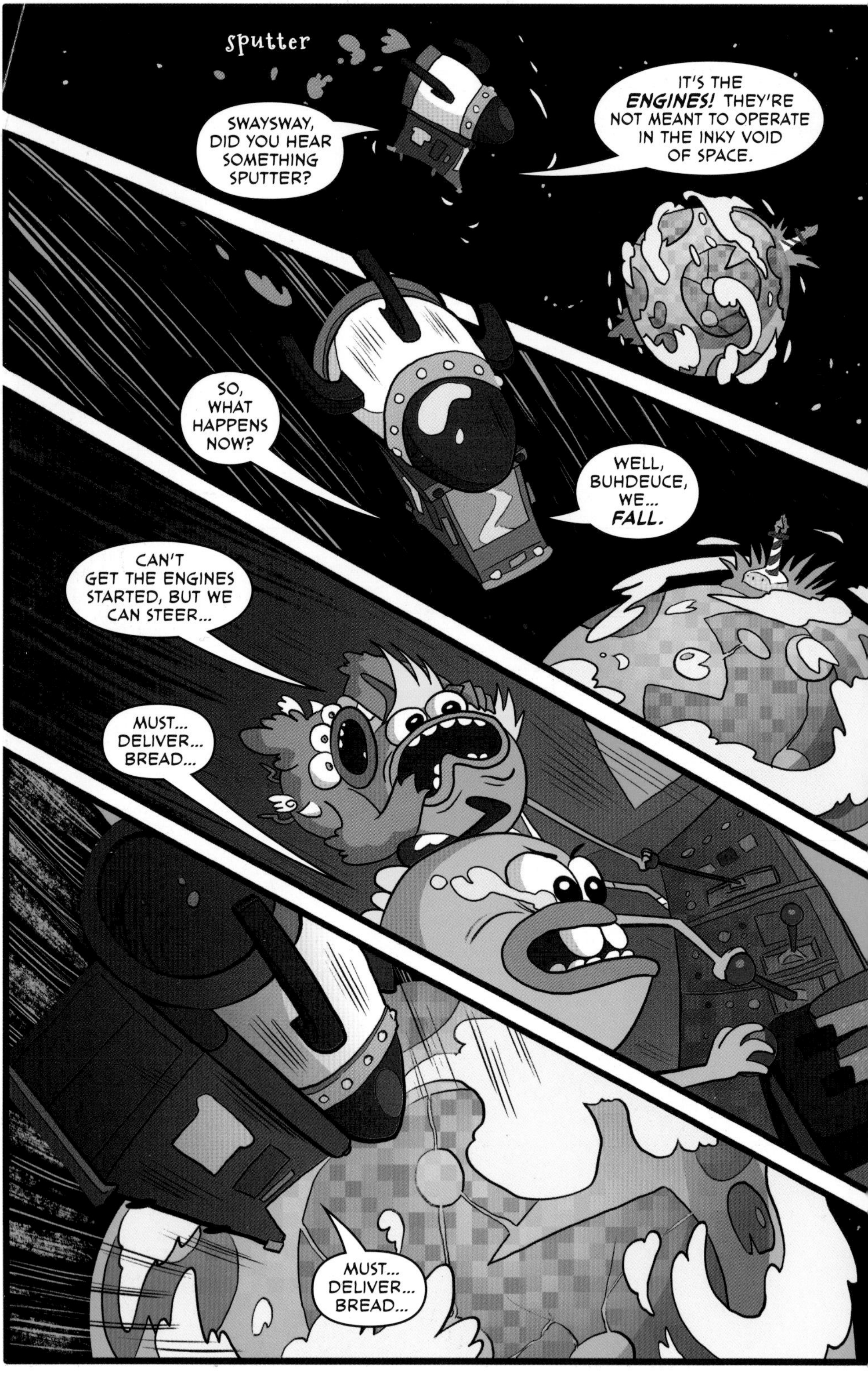
sputter
SWAYSWAY, DID YOU HEAR SOMETHING SPUTTER?
IT'S THE ENGINES! THEY'RE NOT MEANT TO OPERATE IN THE INKY VOID OF SPACE.
SO, WHAT HAPPENS NOW?
WELL, BUHDEUCE, WE... FALL.
CAN'T GET THE ENGINES STARTED, BUT WE CAN STEER...
MUST... DELIVER... BREAD...
MUST... DELIVER... BREAD...

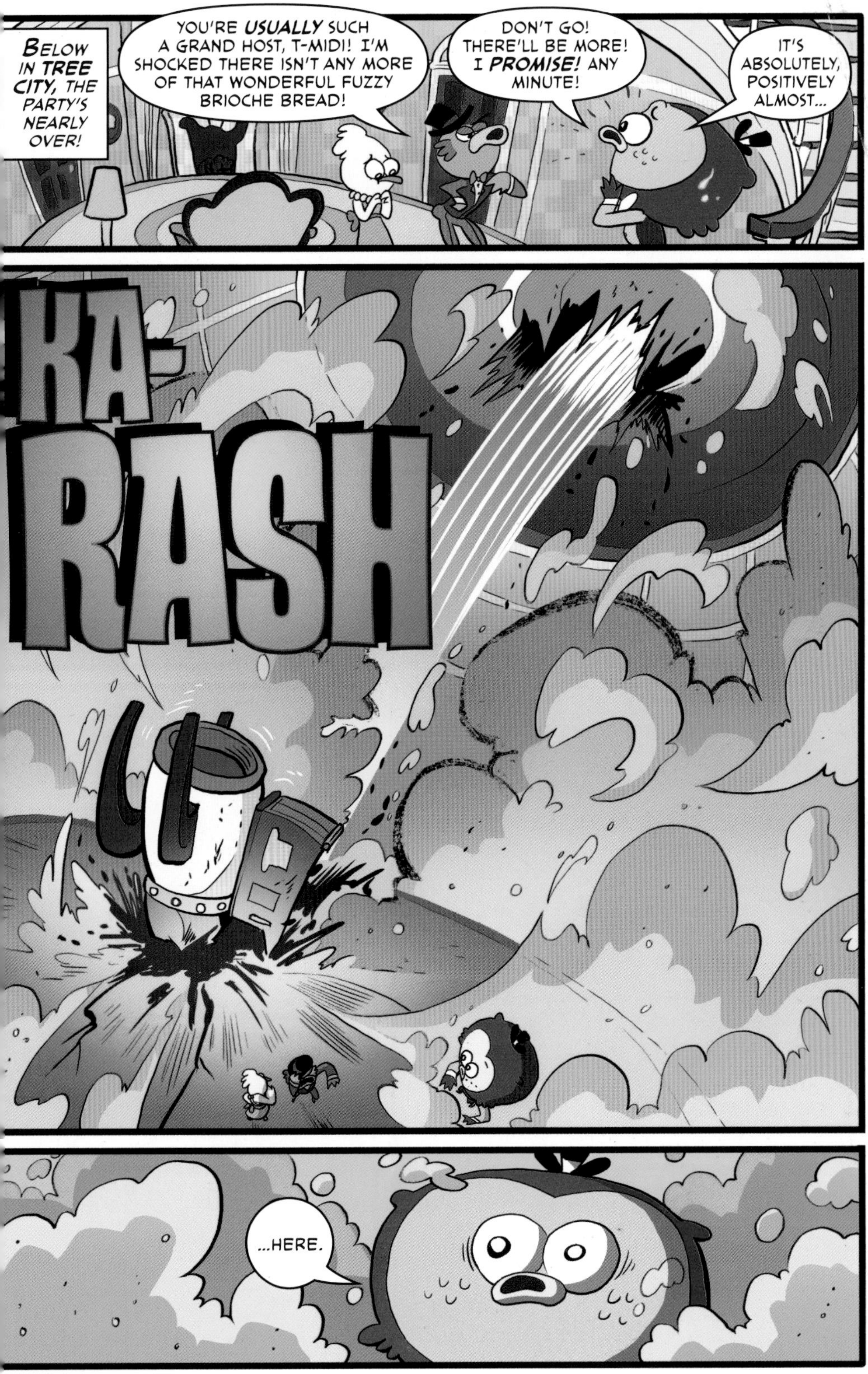
BELOW IN TREE CITY, THE PARTY'S NEARLY OVER!
YOU'RE USUALLY SUCH A GRAND HOST, T-MIDI! I'M SHOCKED THERE ISN'T ANY MORE OF THAT WONDERFUL FUZZY BRIOCHE BREAD!
DON'T GO! THERE'LL BE MORE! I PROMISE! ANY MINUTE!
IT'S ABSOLUTELY, POSITIVELY ALMOST...
KA-RASH
...HERE.

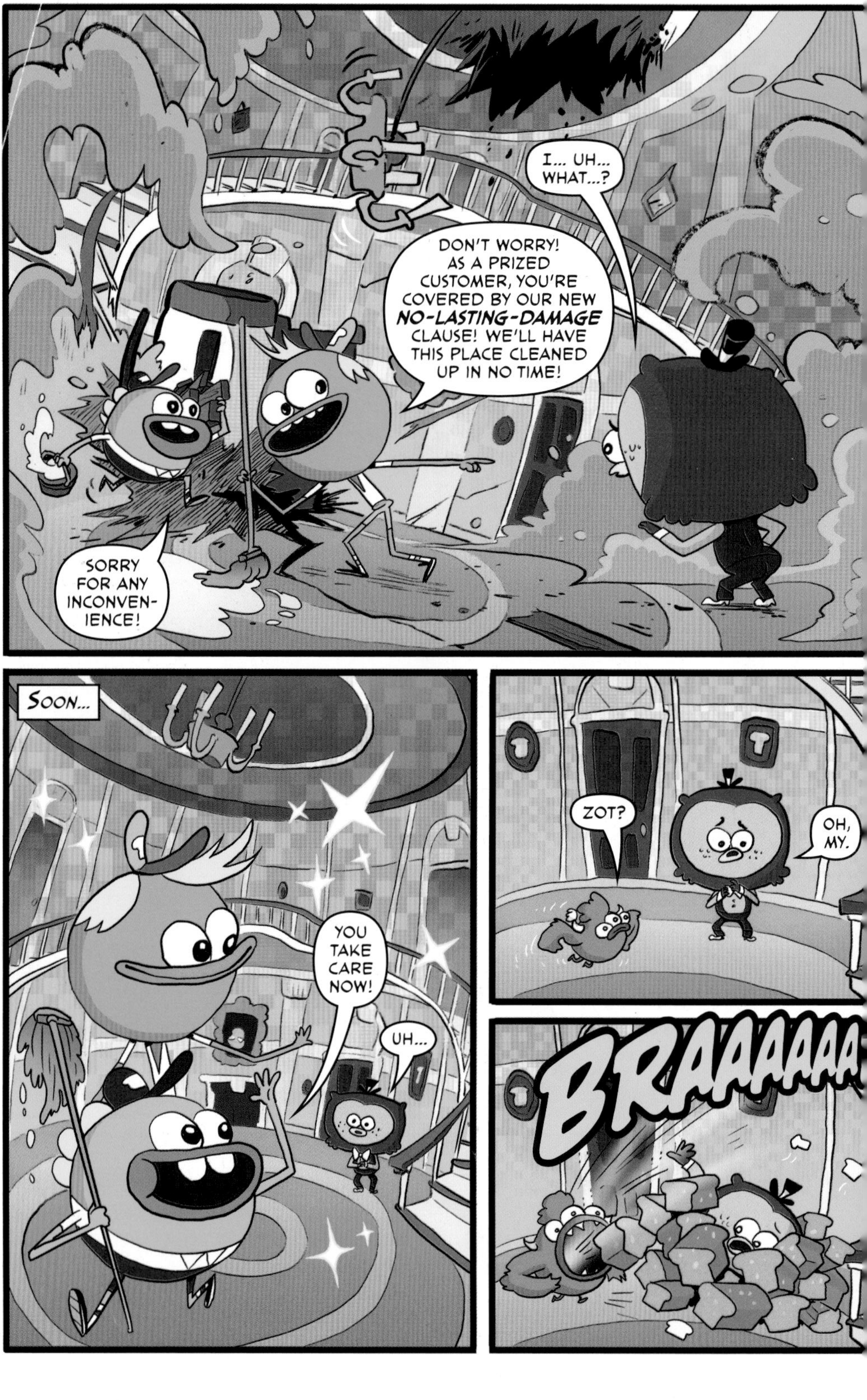
I... UH... WHAT...?
DON'T WORRY! AS A PRIZED CUSTOMER, YOU'RE COVERED BY OUR NEW ***NO-LASTING-DAMAGE*** CLAUSE! WE'LL HAVE THIS PLACE CLEANED UP IN NO TIME!
SORRY FOR ANY INCONVEN-IENCE!
SOON...
YOU TAKE CARE NOW!
UH...
ZOT?
OH, MY.
BRAAAAAA

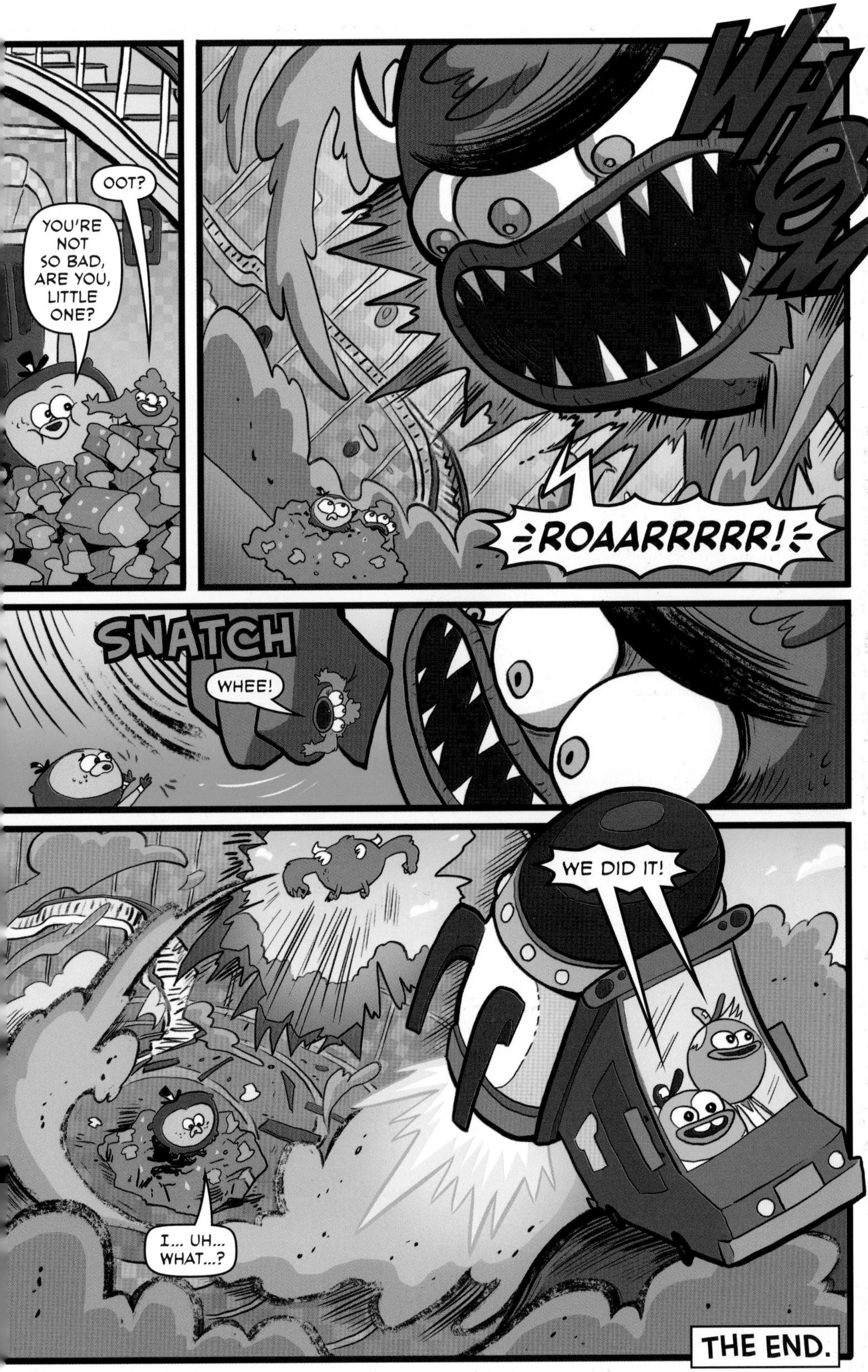
OOT?
YOU'RE NOT SO BAD, ARE YOU, LITTLE ONE?
WHOOM
ROAARRRRR!
SNATCH
WHEE!
WE DID IT!
I... UH... WHAT...?
THE END.

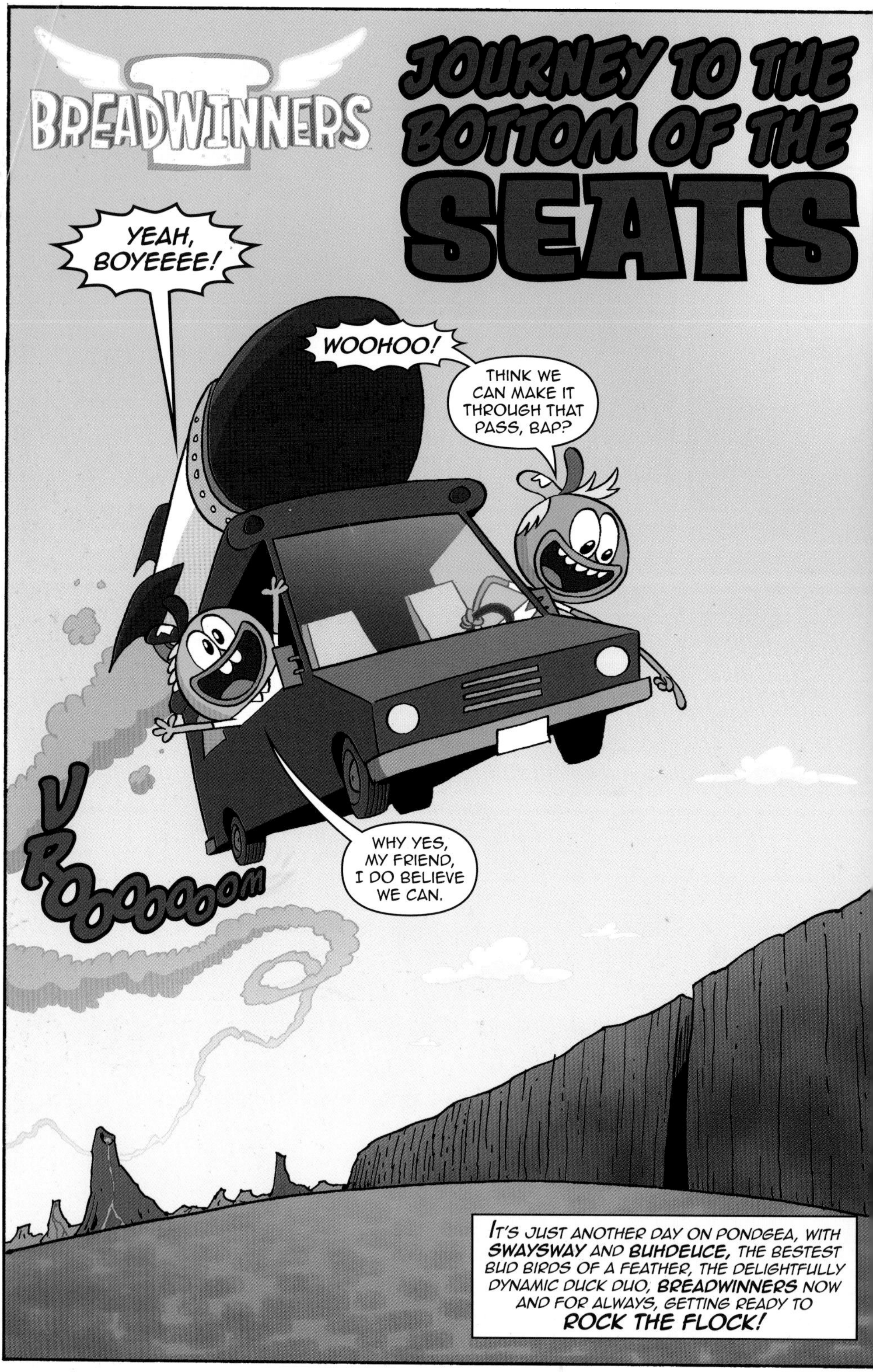
BREADWINNERS
JOURNEY TO THE BOTTOM OF THE SEATS
YEAH, BOYEEEE!
WOOHOO!
THINK WE CAN MAKE IT THROUGH THAT PASS, BAP?
WHY YES, MY FRIEND, I DO BELIEVE WE CAN.
VROOOOOOOOM
IT'S JUST ANOTHER DAY ON PONDGEA, WITH SWAYSWAY AND BUHDEUCE, THE BESTEST BUD BIRDS OF A FEATHER, THE DELIGHTFULLY DYNAMIC DUCK DUO, BREADWINNERS NOW AND FOR ALWAYS, GETTING READY TO ROCK THE FLOCK!

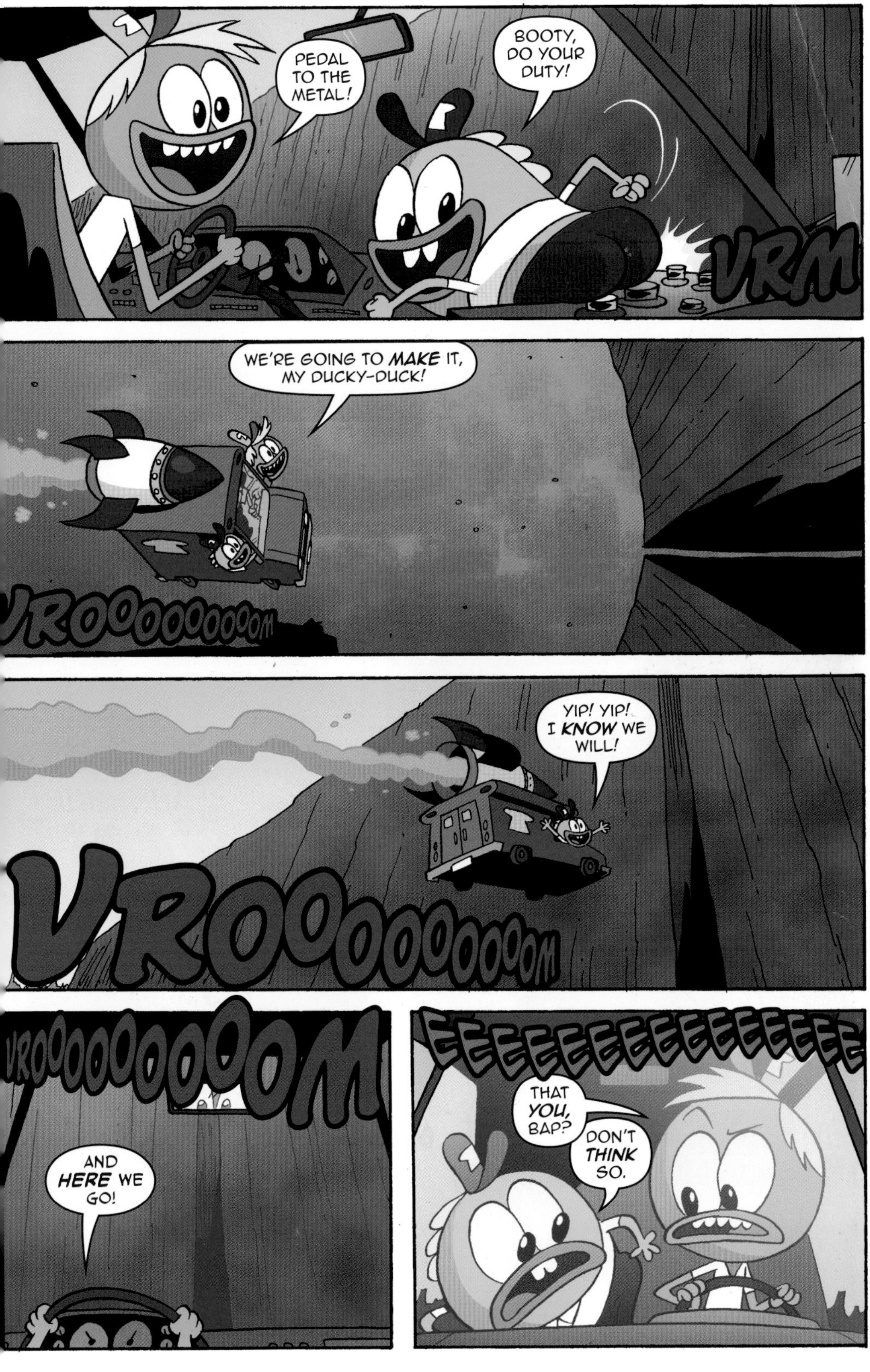
PEDAL TO THE METAL!
BOOTY, DO YOUR DUTY!
VRM
WE'RE GOING TO MAKE IT, MY DUCKY-DUCK!
VROOOOOOOOOM
YIP! YIP! I KNOW WE WILL!
VROOOOOOOOOOM
VROOOOOOOOOOM
AND HERE WE GO!
EEEEEEEEEEEEEEEE
THAT YOU, BAP?
DON'T THINK SO.

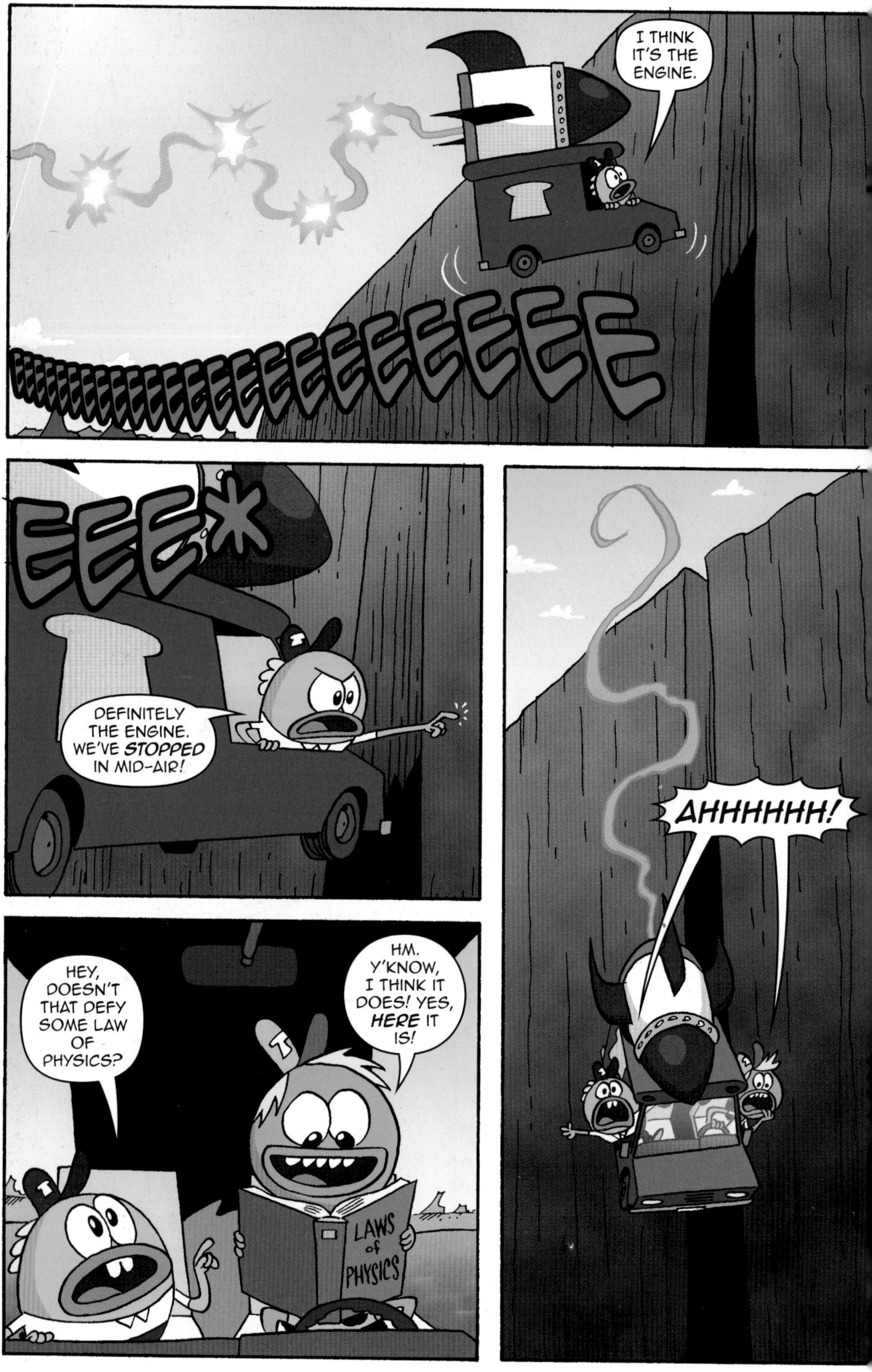
I THINK IT'S THE ENGINE.
EEEEEEEEEEEEEEEEEEEEEEEEEE
EEE*
DEFINITELY THE ENGINE. WE'VE STOPPED IN MID-AIR!
HEY, DOESN'T THAT DEFY SOME LAW OF PHYSICS?
HM. Y'KNOW, I THINK IT DOES! YES, HERE IT IS!
LAWS of PHYSICS
AHHHHHH!

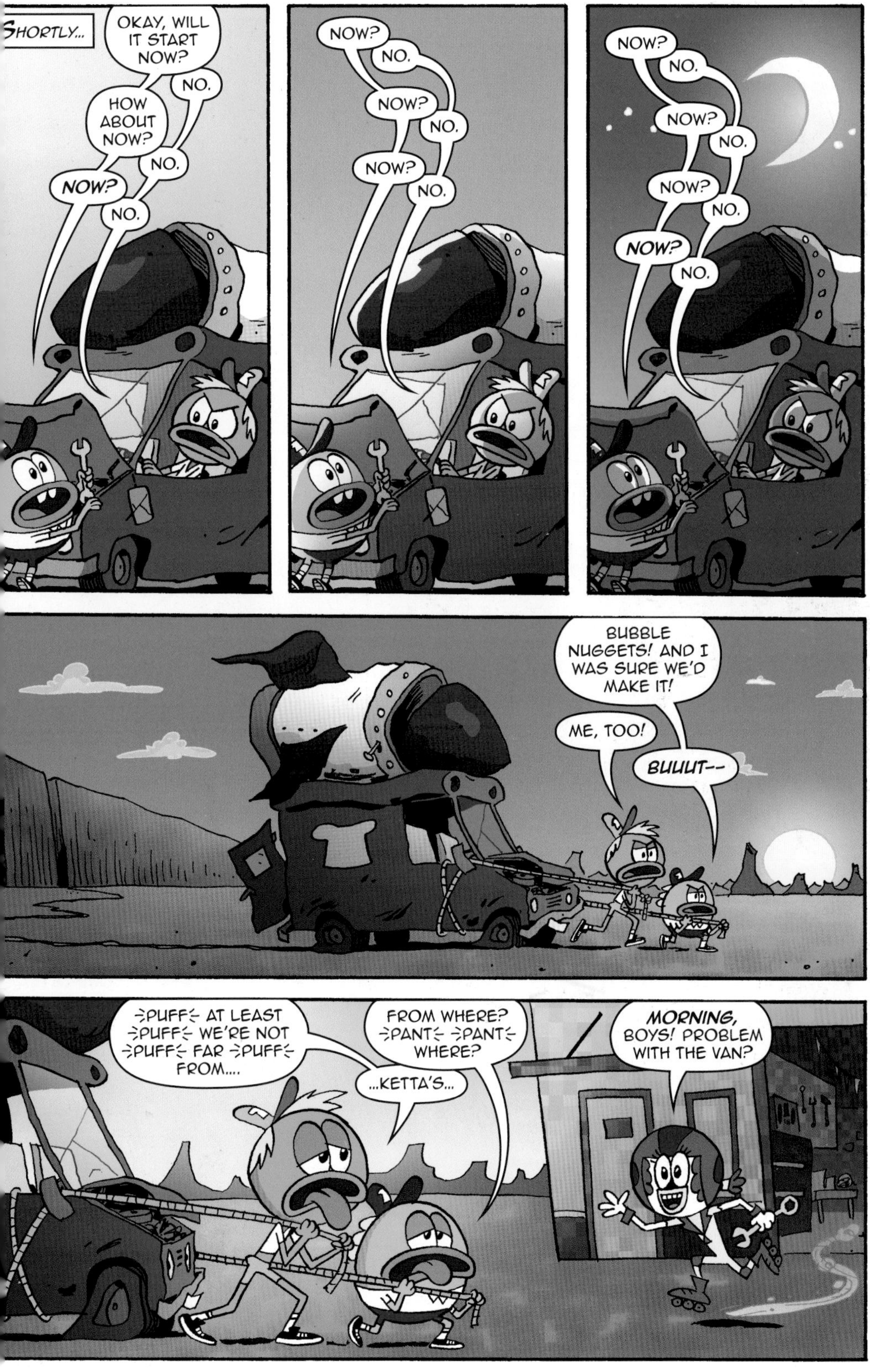
SHORTLY...
OKAY, WILL IT START NOW?
NO.
HOW ABOUT NOW?
NO.
NOW?
NO.
NOW?
NO.
NOW?
NO.
NOW?
NO.
NOW?
NO.
NOW?
NO.
NOW?
NO.
NOW?
NO.
BUBBLE NUGGETS! AND I WAS SURE WE'D MAKE IT!
ME, TOO!
BUUUT--
⸗PUFF⸗ AT LEAST ⸗PUFF⸗ WE'RE NOT ⸗PUFF⸗ FAR ⸗PUFF⸗ FROM....
FROM WHERE? ⸗PANT⸗ ⸗PANT⸗ WHERE?
...KETTA'S...
MORNING, BOYS! PROBLEM WITH THE VAN?

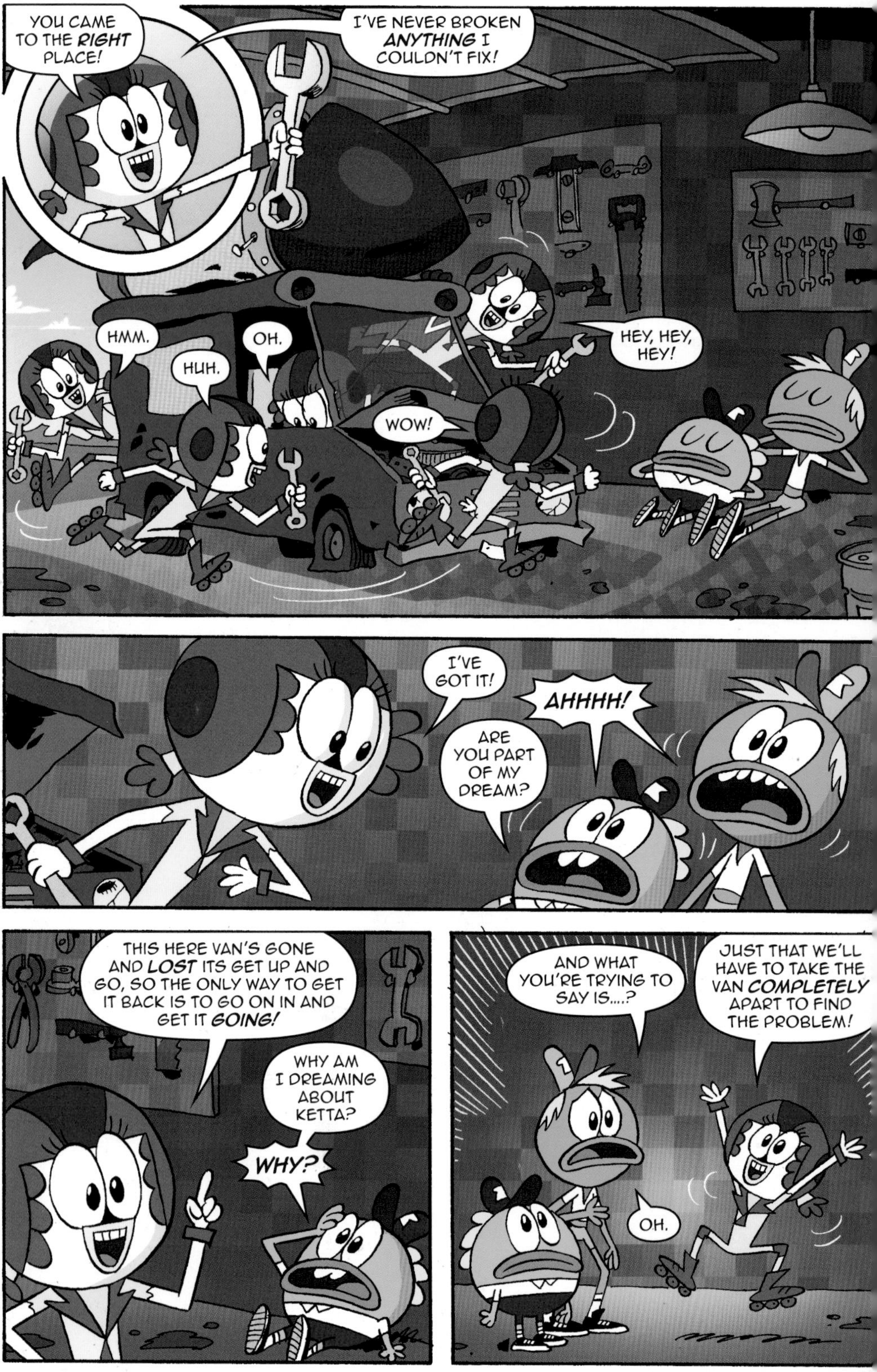
YOU CAME TO THE *RIGHT* PLACE!
I'VE NEVER BROKEN *ANYTHING* I COULDN'T FIX!
HMM.
HUH.
OH.
HEY, HEY, HEY!
WOW!
I'VE GOT IT!
AHHHH!
ARE YOU PART OF MY DREAM?
THIS HERE VAN'S GONE AND *LOST* ITS GET UP AND GO, SO THE ONLY WAY TO GET IT BACK IS TO GO ON IN AND GET IT *GOING!*
WHY AM I DREAMING ABOUT KETTA?
WHY?
AND WHAT YOU'RE TRYING TO SAY IS....?
JUST THAT WE'LL HAVE TO TAKE THE VAN *COMPLETELY* APART TO FIND THE PROBLEM!
OH.

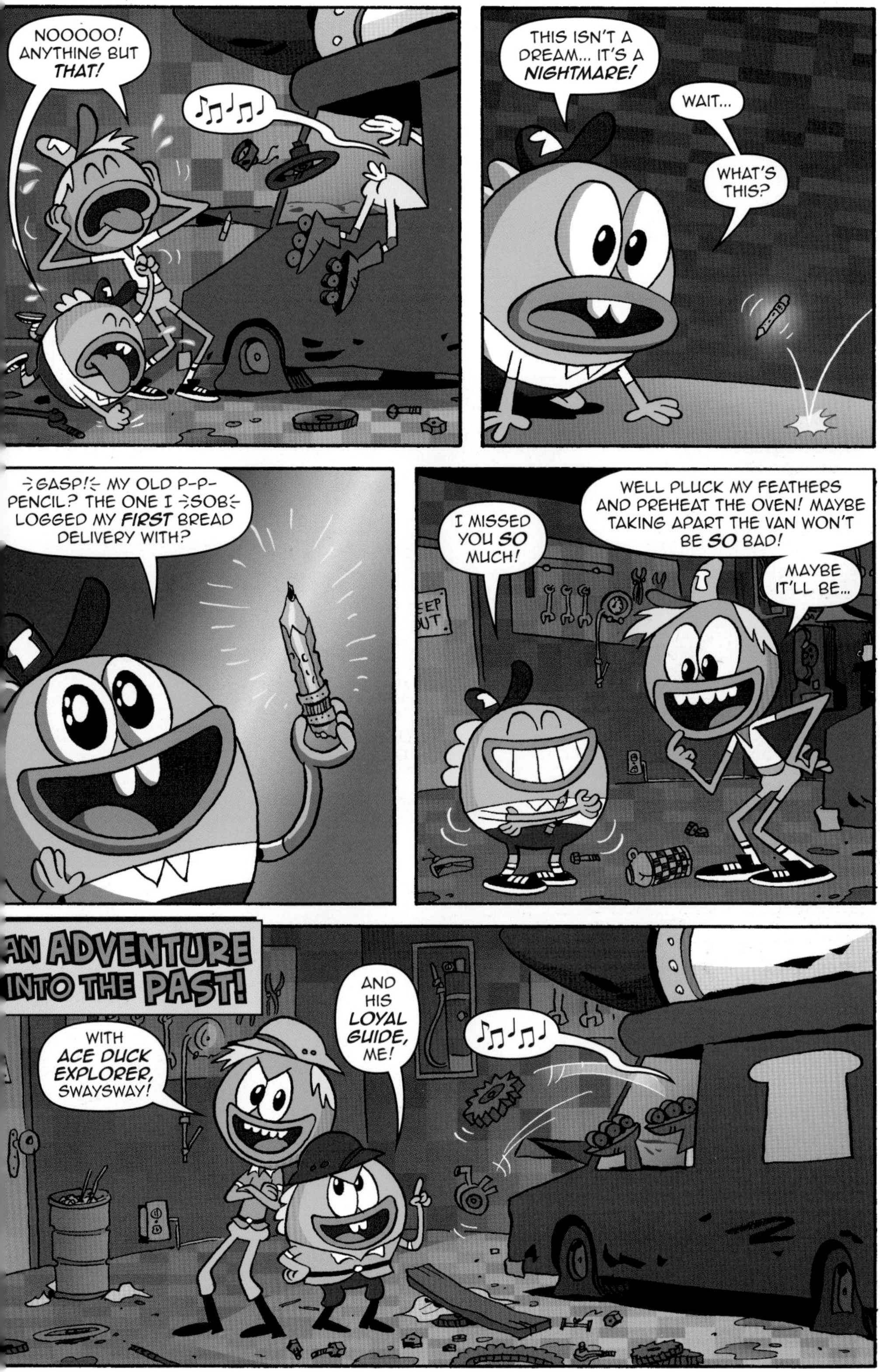
NOOOOO! ANYTHING BUT THAT!
♪♫♩♫♩
THIS ISN'T A DREAM... IT'S A NIGHTMARE!
WAIT...
WHAT'S THIS?
⇒GASP!⇐ MY OLD P-P-PENCIL? THE ONE I ⇒SOB⇐ LOGGED MY FIRST BREAD DELIVERY WITH?
I MISSED YOU SO MUCH!
WELL PLUCK MY FEATHERS AND PREHEAT THE OVEN! MAYBE TAKING APART THE VAN WON'T BE SO BAD!
MAYBE IT'LL BE...
AN ADVENTURE INTO THE PAST!
WITH ACE DUCK EXPLORER, SWAYSWAY!
AND HIS LOYAL GUIDE, ME!
♪♫♩♫♩

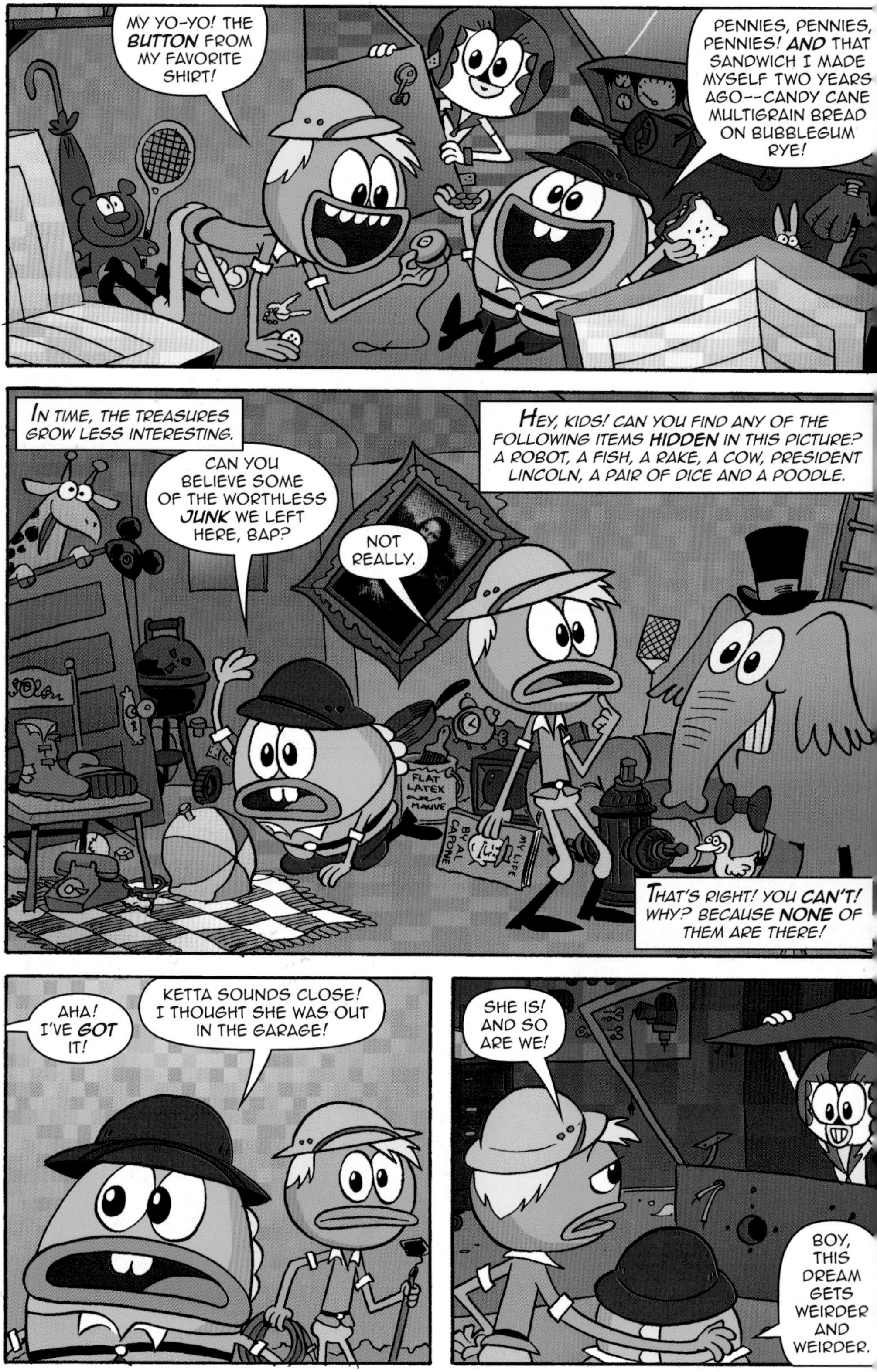
MY YO-YO! THE BUTTON FROM MY FAVORITE SHIRT!
PENNIES, PENNIES, PENNIES! AND THAT SANDWICH I MADE MYSELF TWO YEARS AGO--CANDY CANE MULTIGRAIN BREAD ON BUBBLEGUM RYE!
IN TIME, THE TREASURES GROW LESS INTERESTING.
HEY, KIDS! CAN YOU FIND ANY OF THE FOLLOWING ITEMS HIDDEN IN THIS PICTURE? A ROBOT, A FISH, A RAKE, A COW, PRESIDENT LINCOLN, A PAIR OF DICE AND A POODLE.
CAN YOU BELIEVE SOME OF THE WORTHLESS JUNK WE LEFT HERE, BAP?
NOT REALLY.
FLAT LATEX MAUVE
MY LIFE BY AL CAPONE
THAT'S RIGHT! YOU CAN'T! WHY? BECAUSE NONE OF THEM ARE THERE!
AHA! I'VE GOT IT!
KETTA SOUNDS CLOSE! I THOUGHT SHE WAS OUT IN THE GARAGE!
SHE IS! AND SO ARE WE!
BOY, THIS DREAM GETS WEIRDER AND WEIRDER.

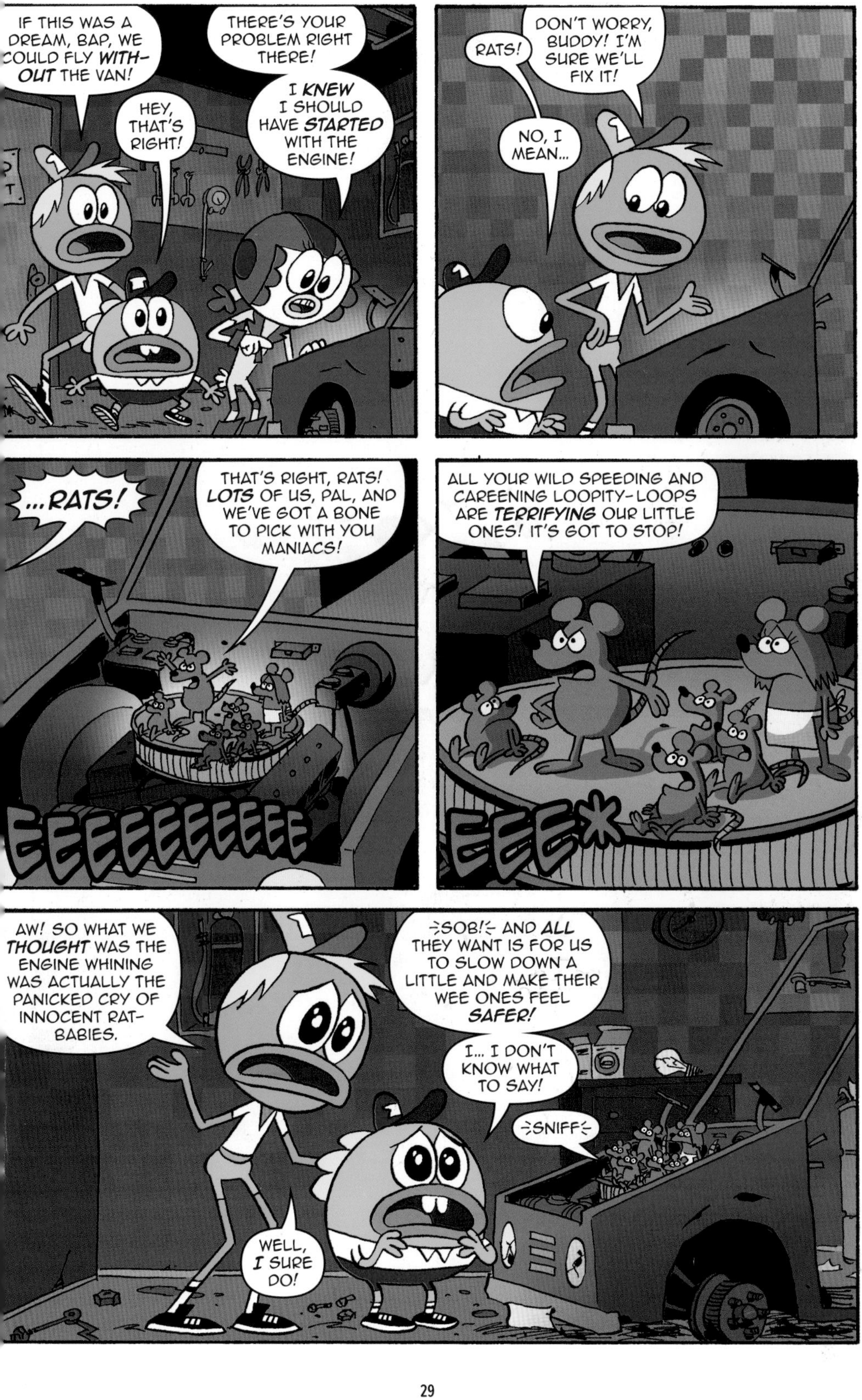

IF THIS WAS A DREAM, BAP, WE COULD FLY WITH-OUT THE VAN!
HEY, THAT'S RIGHT!
THERE'S YOUR PROBLEM RIGHT THERE!
I KNEW I SHOULD HAVE STARTED WITH THE ENGINE!
RATS!
DON'T WORRY, BUDDY! I'M SURE WE'LL FIX IT!
NO, I MEAN...
...RATS!
THAT'S RIGHT, RATS! LOTS OF US, PAL, AND WE'VE GOT A BONE TO PICK WITH YOU MANIACS!
EEEEEEEEEE
ALL YOUR WILD SPEEDING AND CAREENING LOOPITY-LOOPS ARE TERRIFYING OUR LITTLE ONES! IT'S GOT TO STOP!
EEE*
AW! SO WHAT WE THOUGHT WAS THE ENGINE WHINING WAS ACTUALLY THE PANICKED CRY OF INNOCENT RAT-BABIES.
SOB! AND ALL THEY WANT IS FOR US TO SLOW DOWN A LITTLE AND MAKE THEIR WEE ONES FEEL SAFER!
I... I DON'T KNOW WHAT TO SAY!
SNIFF
WELL, I SURE DO!

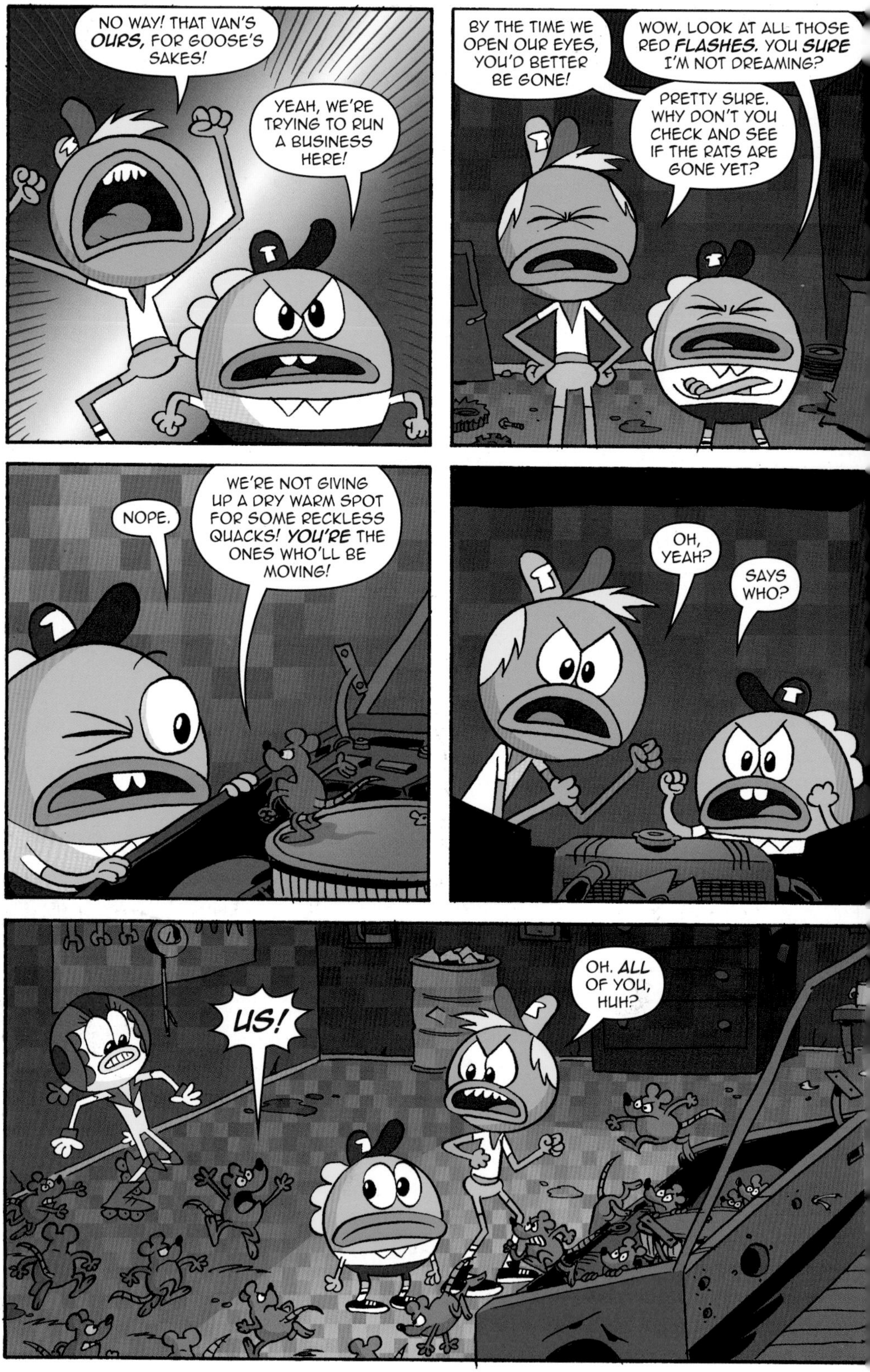
NO WAY! THAT VAN'S OURS, FOR GOOSE'S SAKES!
YEAH, WE'RE TRYING TO RUN A BUSINESS HERE!
BY THE TIME WE OPEN OUR EYES, YOU'D BETTER BE GONE!
WOW, LOOK AT ALL THOSE RED FLASHES. YOU SURE I'M NOT DREAMING?
PRETTY SURE. WHY DON'T YOU CHECK AND SEE IF THE RATS ARE GONE YET?
NOPE.
WE'RE NOT GIVING UP A DRY WARM SPOT FOR SOME RECKLESS QUACKS! YOU'RE THE ONES WHO'LL BE MOVING!
OH, YEAH?
SAYS WHO?
US!
OH. ALL OF YOU, HUH?

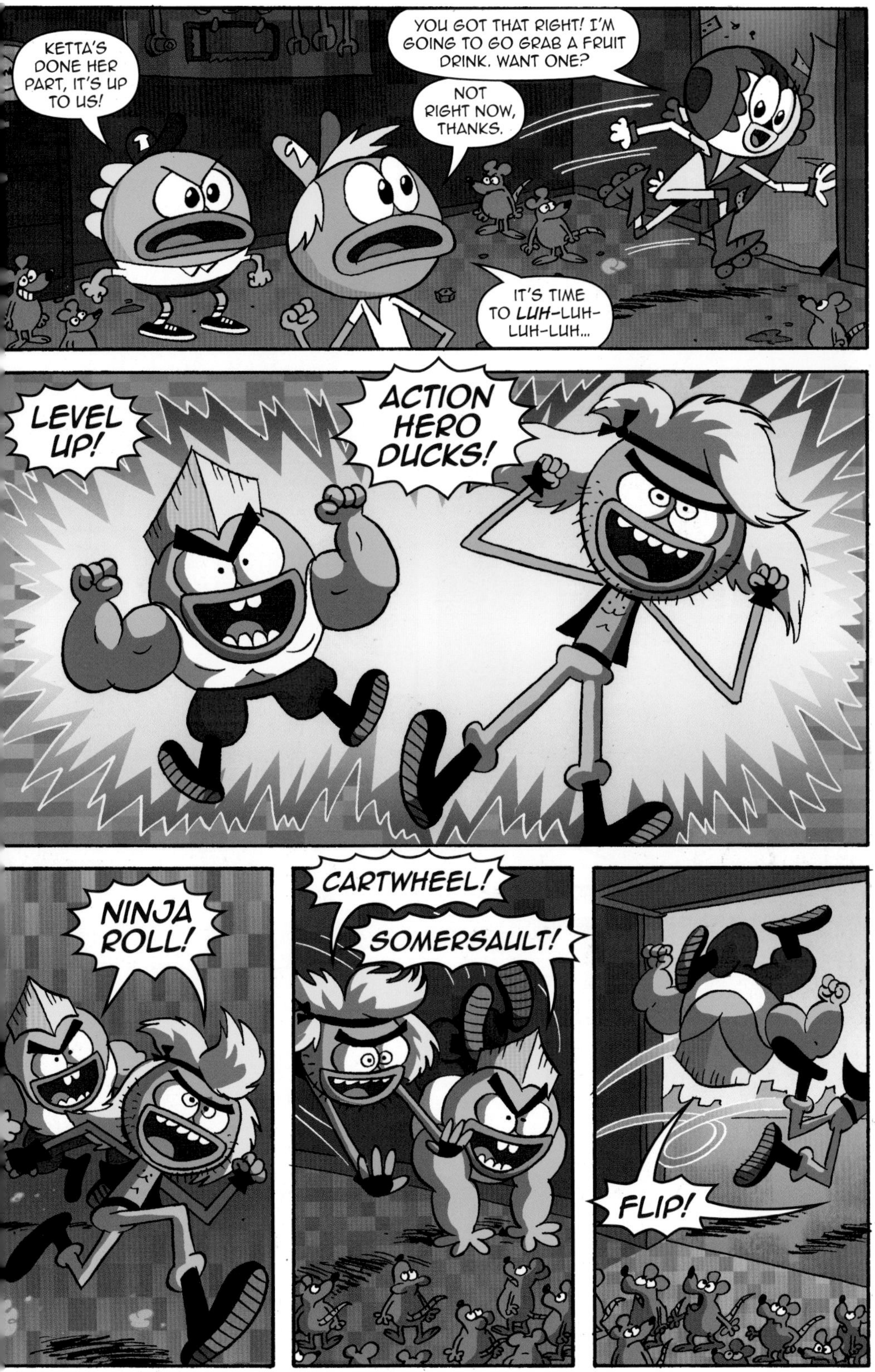
KETTA'S DONE HER PART, IT'S UP TO US!
YOU GOT THAT RIGHT! I'M GOING TO GO GRAB A FRUIT DRINK. WANT ONE?
NOT RIGHT NOW, THANKS.
IT'S TIME TO LUH-LUH-LUH-LUH...
LEVEL UP!
ACTION HERO DUCKS!
NINJA ROLL!
CARTWHEEL!
SOMERSAULT!
FLIP!

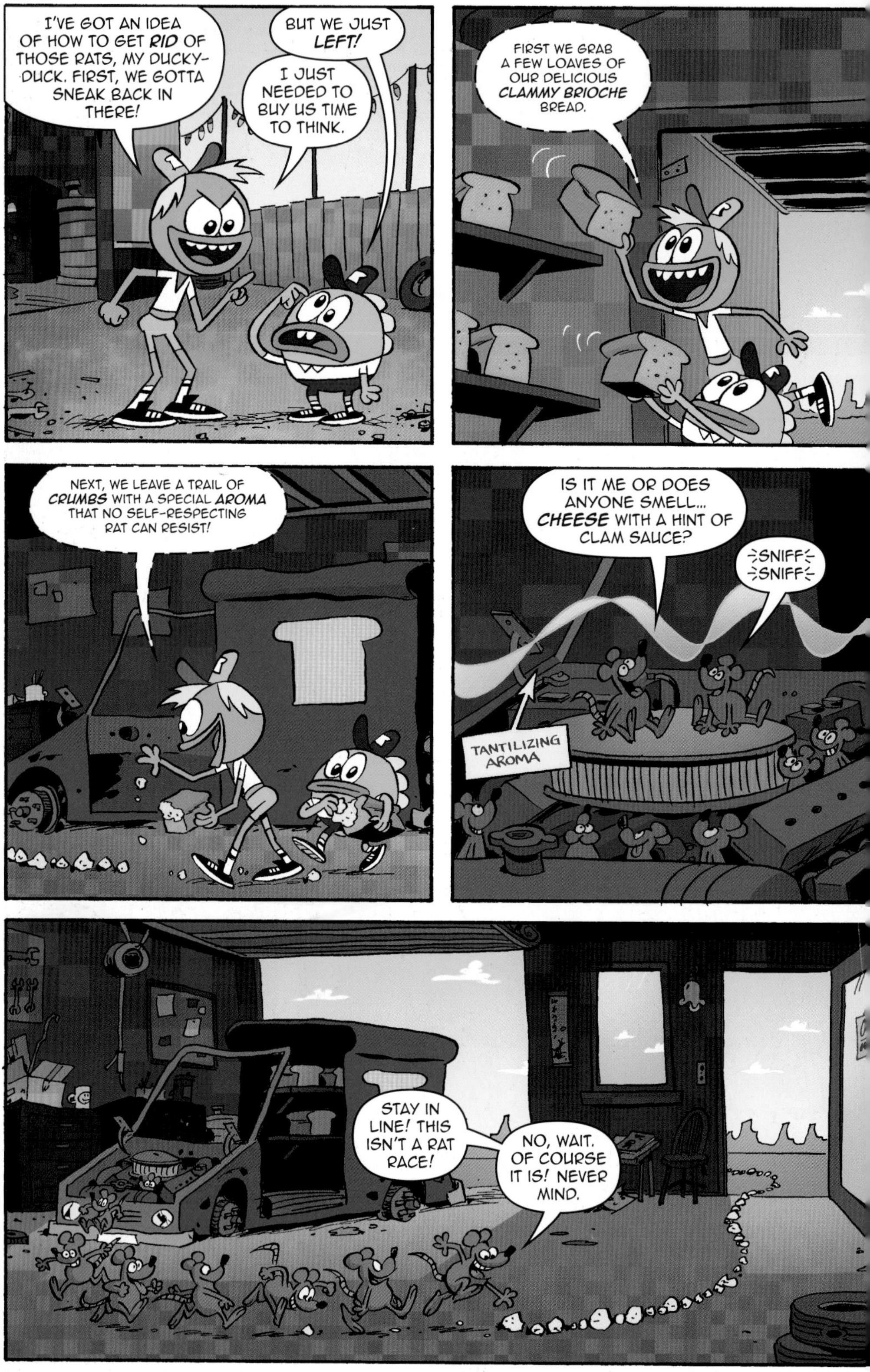
I'VE GOT AN IDEA OF HOW TO GET RID OF THOSE RATS, MY DUCKY-DUCK. FIRST, WE GOTTA SNEAK BACK IN THERE!
BUT WE JUST LEFT!
I JUST NEEDED TO BUY US TIME TO THINK.
FIRST WE GRAB A FEW LOAVES OF OUR DELICIOUS CLAMMY BRIOCHE BREAD.
NEXT, WE LEAVE A TRAIL OF CRUMBS WITH A SPECIAL AROMA THAT NO SELF-RESPECTING RAT CAN RESIST!
IS IT ME OR DOES ANYONE SMELL... CHEESE WITH A HINT OF CLAM SAUCE?
SNIFF SNIFF
TANTILIZING AROMA
STAY IN LINE! THIS ISN'T A RAT RACE!
NO, WAIT. OF COURSE IT IS! NEVER MIND.

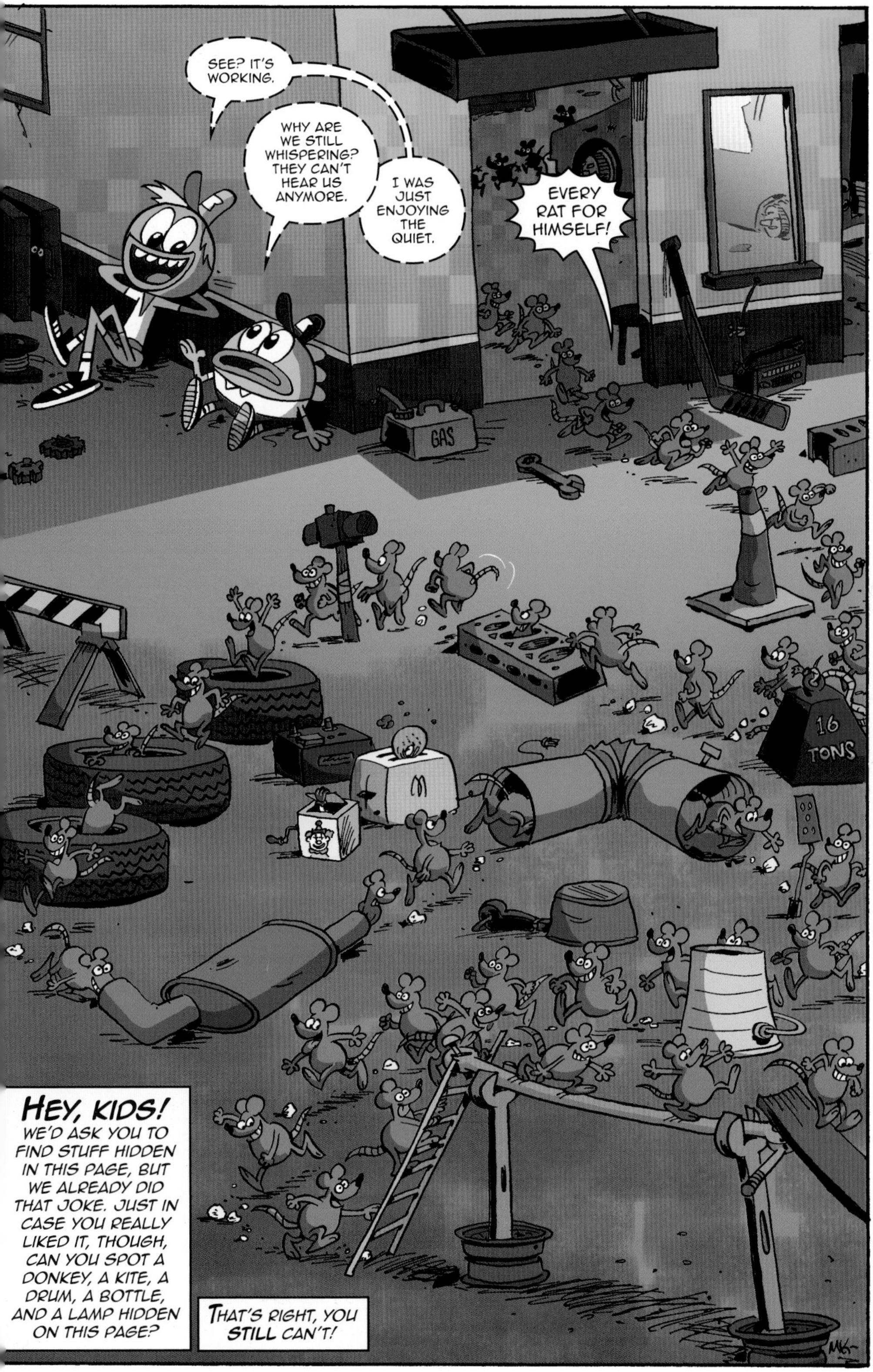
SEE? IT'S WORKING.
WHY ARE WE STILL WHISPERING? THEY CAN'T HEAR US ANYMORE.
I WAS JUST ENJOYING THE QUIET.
EVERY RAT FOR HIMSELF!
GAS
16 TONS
HEY, KIDS! WE'D ASK YOU TO FIND STUFF HIDDEN IN THIS PAGE, BUT WE ALREADY DID THAT JOKE. JUST IN CASE YOU REALLY LIKED IT, THOUGH, CAN YOU SPOT A DONKEY, A KITE, A DRUM, A BOTTLE, AND A LAMP HIDDEN ON THIS PAGE?
THAT'S RIGHT, YOU STILL CAN'T!

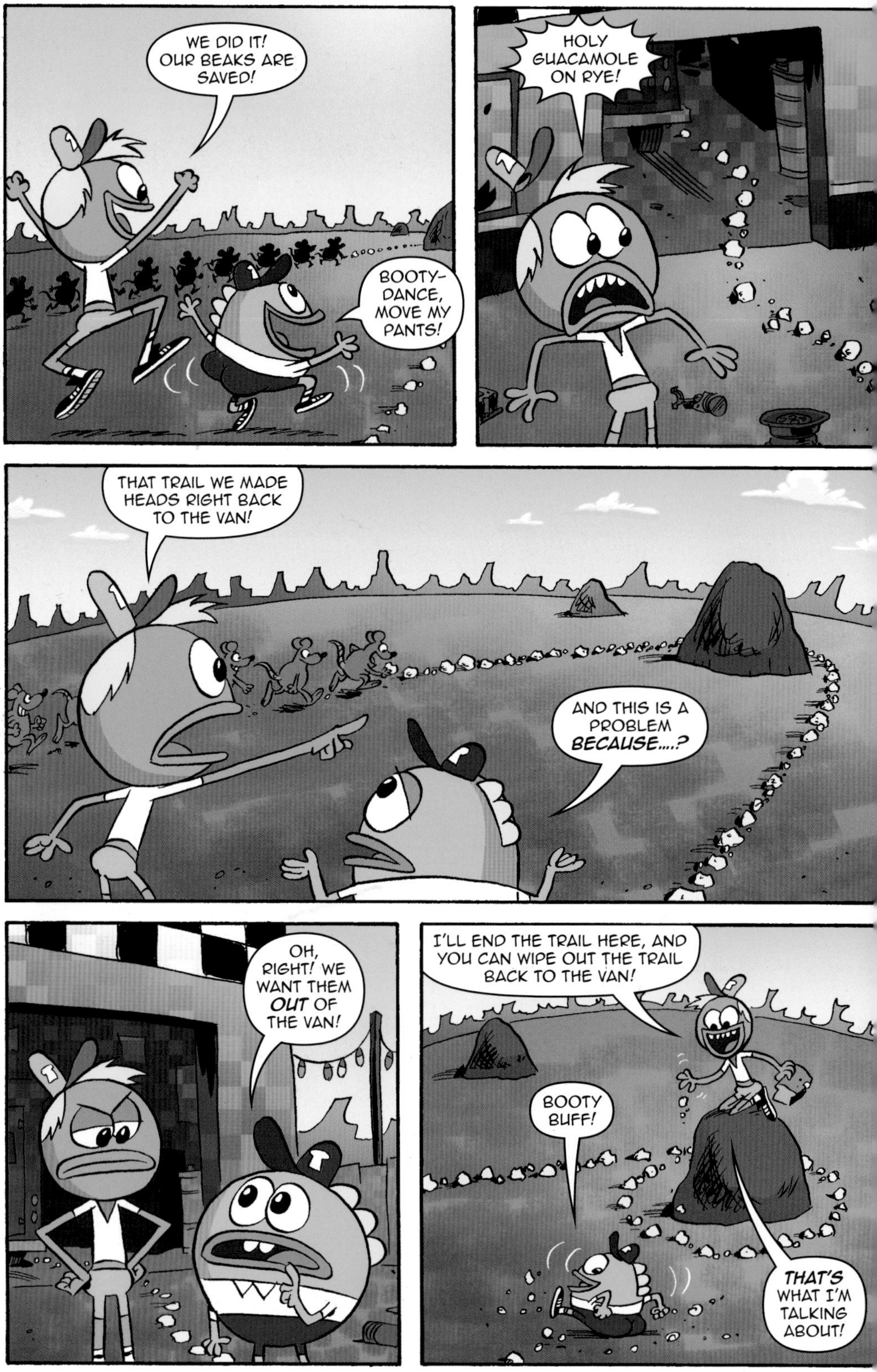

WE DID IT! OUR BEAKS ARE SAVED!
BOOTY-DANCE, MOVE MY PANTS!
HOLY GUACAMOLE ON RYE!
THAT TRAIL WE MADE HEADS RIGHT BACK TO THE VAN!
AND THIS IS A PROBLEM *BECAUSE*.....?
OH, RIGHT! WE WANT THEM *OUT* OF THE VAN!
I'LL END THE TRAIL HERE, AND YOU CAN WIPE OUT THE TRAIL BACK TO THE VAN!
BOOTY BUFF!
THAT'S WHAT I'M TALKING ABOUT!

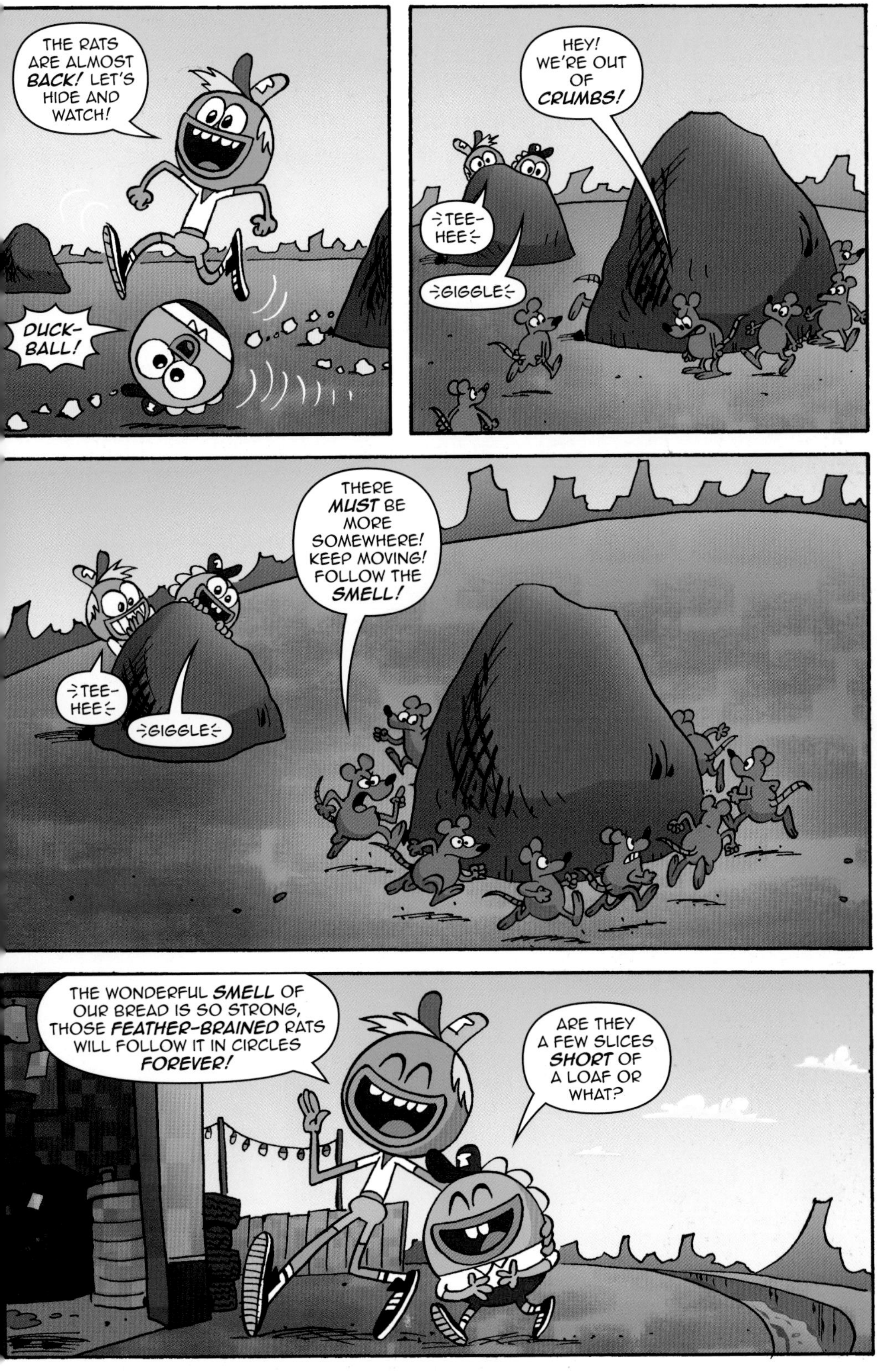
THE RATS ARE ALMOST BACK! LET'S HIDE AND WATCH!
DUCK-BALL!
HEY! WE'RE OUT OF CRUMBS!
TEE-HEE
GIGGLE
THERE MUST BE MORE SOMEWHERE! KEEP MOVING! FOLLOW THE SMELL!
TEE-HEE
GIGGLE
THE WONDERFUL SMELL OF OUR BREAD IS SO STRONG, THOSE FEATHER-BRAINED RATS WILL FOLLOW IT IN CIRCLES FOREVER!
ARE THEY A FEW SLICES SHORT OF A LOAF OR WHAT?

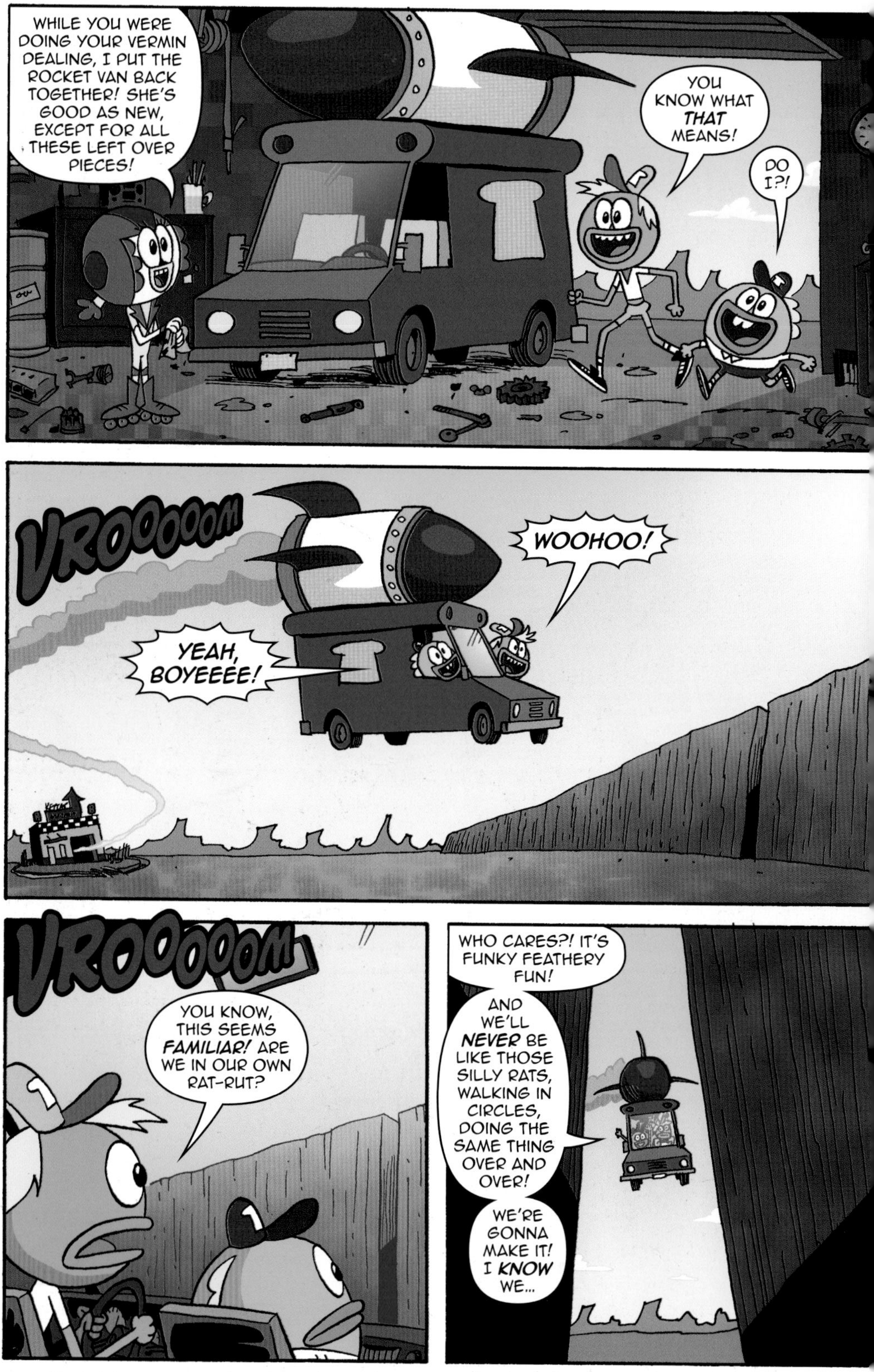
WHILE YOU WERE DOING YOUR VERMIN DEALING, I PUT THE ROCKET VAN BACK TOGETHER! SHE'S GOOD AS NEW, EXCEPT FOR ALL THESE LEFT OVER PIECES!
YOU KNOW WHAT *THAT* MEANS!
DO I?!
VROOOOOM
WOOHOO!
YEAH, BOYEEEE!
VROOOOOM
YOU KNOW, THIS SEEMS *FAMILIAR!* ARE WE IN OUR OWN RAT-RUT?
WHO CARES?! IT'S FUNKY FEATHERY FUN!
AND WE'LL *NEVER* BE LIKE THOSE SILLY RATS, WALKING IN CIRCLES, DOING THE SAME THING OVER AND OVER!
WE'RE GONNA MAKE IT! I *KNOW* WE...

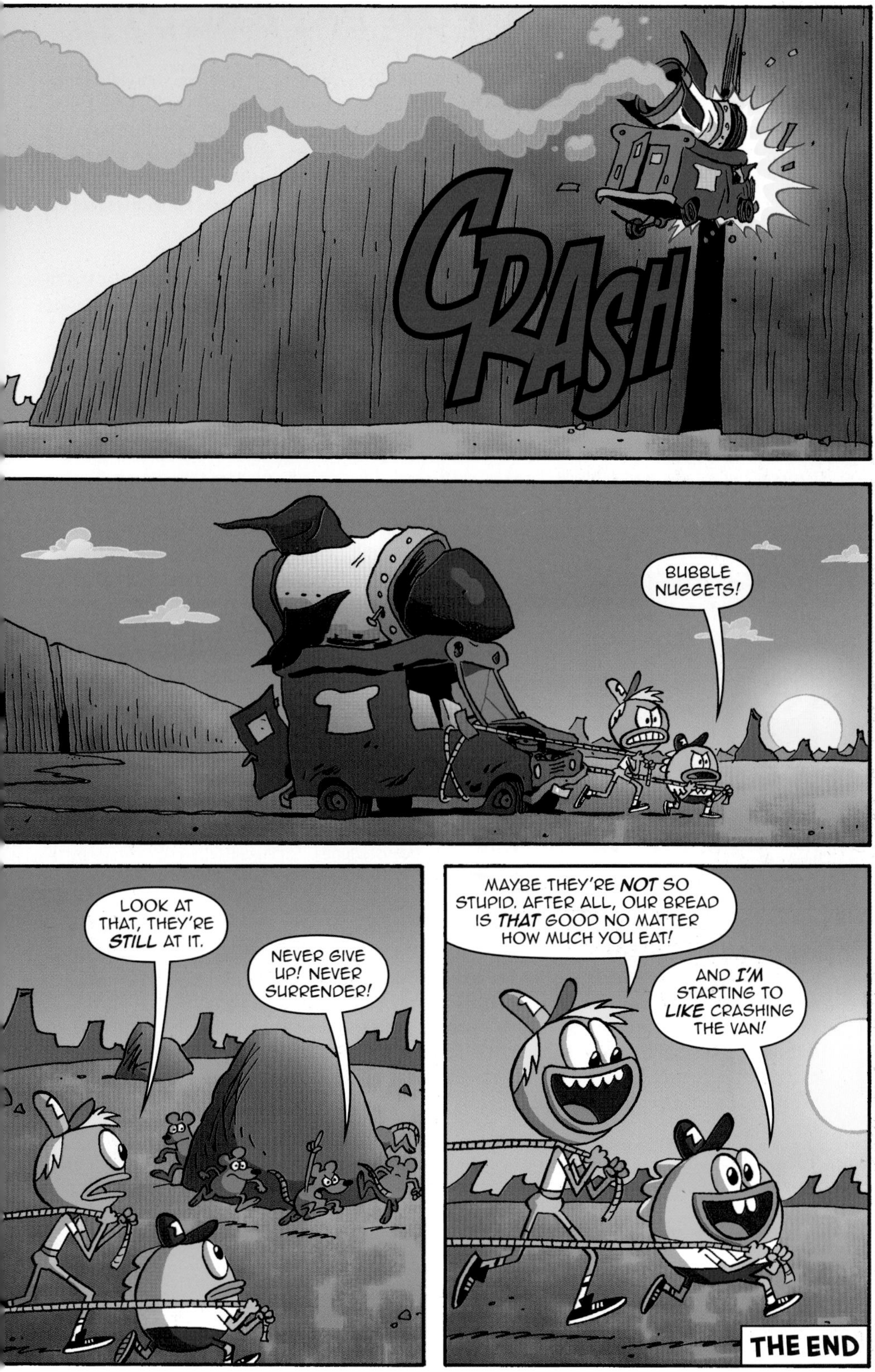
CRASH
BUBBLE NUGGETS!
LOOK AT THAT, THEY'RE STILL AT IT.
NEVER GIVE UP! NEVER SURRENDER!
MAYBE THEY'RE NOT SO STUPID. AFTER ALL, OUR BREAD IS THAT GOOD NO MATTER HOW MUCH YOU EAT!
AND I'M STARTING TO LIKE CRASHING THE VAN!
THE END

WATCH OUT FOR PAPERCUTZ

Welcome to the fabulous, fat-free, fast-paced, first **BREADWINNERS** graphic novel from Papercutz—those hard-working, enthusiastic, comic-makers dedicated to publishing graphic novels for all ages. I'm Jim Salicrup, the carb-loving Editor-in-Chief, and I'm here to bring you up to speed on what we have planned for the future—and beyond! But as I was writing this page, I suddenly had a touch of déjà vu and realized I said much of this already in our first **SANJAY AND CRAIG** graphic novel (still on sale wherever awesome graphic novels are sold!). So, rather than find a clever way to say everything all over again with different words, I'll just take the easy way out and use most of the same words!

Let's start at the beginning. A little over ten years ago, Papercutz publisher Terry Nantier and I founded this little comicbook company to address a need—there just didn't seem to be enough comics and graphic novels for kids. That was incredibly ironic, since most folks think of comics as being for kids. After ten years of producing all types of comics for all ages, we made an incredible deal with the awesome folks at Nickelodeon to create a line of graphic novels based on their latest and greatest new animated series. This really is a match made in cartoon heaven – Nickelodeon, loved by millions of kids for their brilliant cartoon shows and characters, and Papercutz, the graphic novel publisher devoted to creating the best comics for kids—together at last!

Terry and I, along with Joan Hilty and Linda Lee, got to spend a day at the Nickelodeon Animation Studio where we talked about our plans with the creators of Sanjay and Craig, Breadwinners, and more. Everyone was excited and as thrilled as we were about the characters leaping off the TV screen and onto the comicbook page!

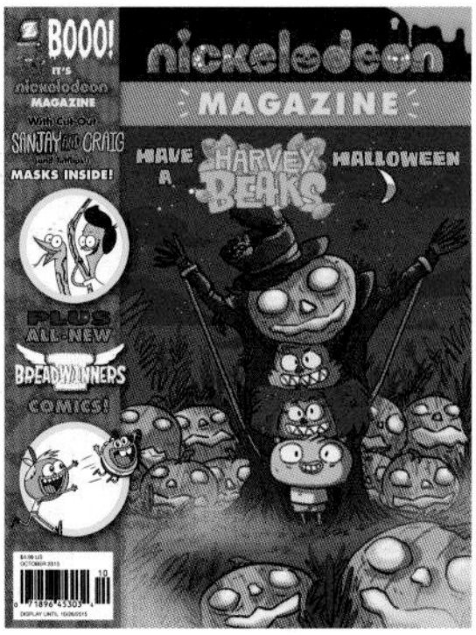
BOOO!
IT'S nickelodeon MAGAZINE
With Cut-Out SANJAY AND CRAIG MASKS INSIDE!
PLUS ALL-NEW BREADWINNERS COMICS!
nickelodeon
MAGAZINE
HAVE A HARVEY BEAKS HALLOWEEN

To kick off this historic publishing partnership, we launched an all-new **NICKELODEON MAGAZINE**, which, in addition to features such as posters, activities, calendars, etc., is jam-packed with comics—the very same comics we'll be collecting in our graphic novels. The magazine is available wherever magazines are sold, and is also available as a subscription. Just go to Papercutz.com/nickmag for all the details.

Editors Michael Petranek and Suzannah Rowntree helped get the comics started, but the bulk of the editorial work was handled by Bethany Bryan (Associate Editor/Papercutz) and Joan Hilty (Comics Editor/Nickelodeon). Together, working with writer Stefan Petrucha, and artists Allison Stejlau and Mike Kazaleh, colorist Laurie E. Smith, and letterer Tom Orzechowski they've come up with the **BREADWINNERS** graphic novel you see before you.

But this is just the beginning! Coming up next will be the premiere **HARVEY BEAKS** graphic novel, followed by the second **SANJAY AND CRAIG** graphic novel, and then that's quickly followed by the debut of the first **PIG GOAT BANANA CRICKET** graphic novel! Is this the Nickelodeon Age of Graphic Novels or what? And the best part is that you are a **BIG** part of it! Tell us what you think of what we're doing—your opinion matters to us. Our goal is to produce graphic novels that you will love as much as the original TV shows. Write to us at the addresses below and tell us if we succeeded or not. We'll be waiting for your comments!

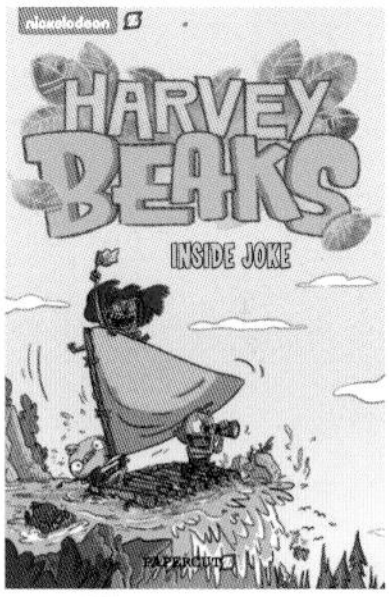
nickelodeon
HARVEY BEAKS
INSIDE JOKE
PAPERCUTZ

Thanks,

Jim

STAY IN TOUCH!

EMAIL:	salicrup@papercutz.com
WEB:	papercutz.com
TWITTER:	@papercutzgn
FACEBOOK:	PAPERCUTZGRAPHICNOVELS
FANMAIL:	Papercutz, 160 Broadway, Suite 700, East Wing, New York, NY 10038

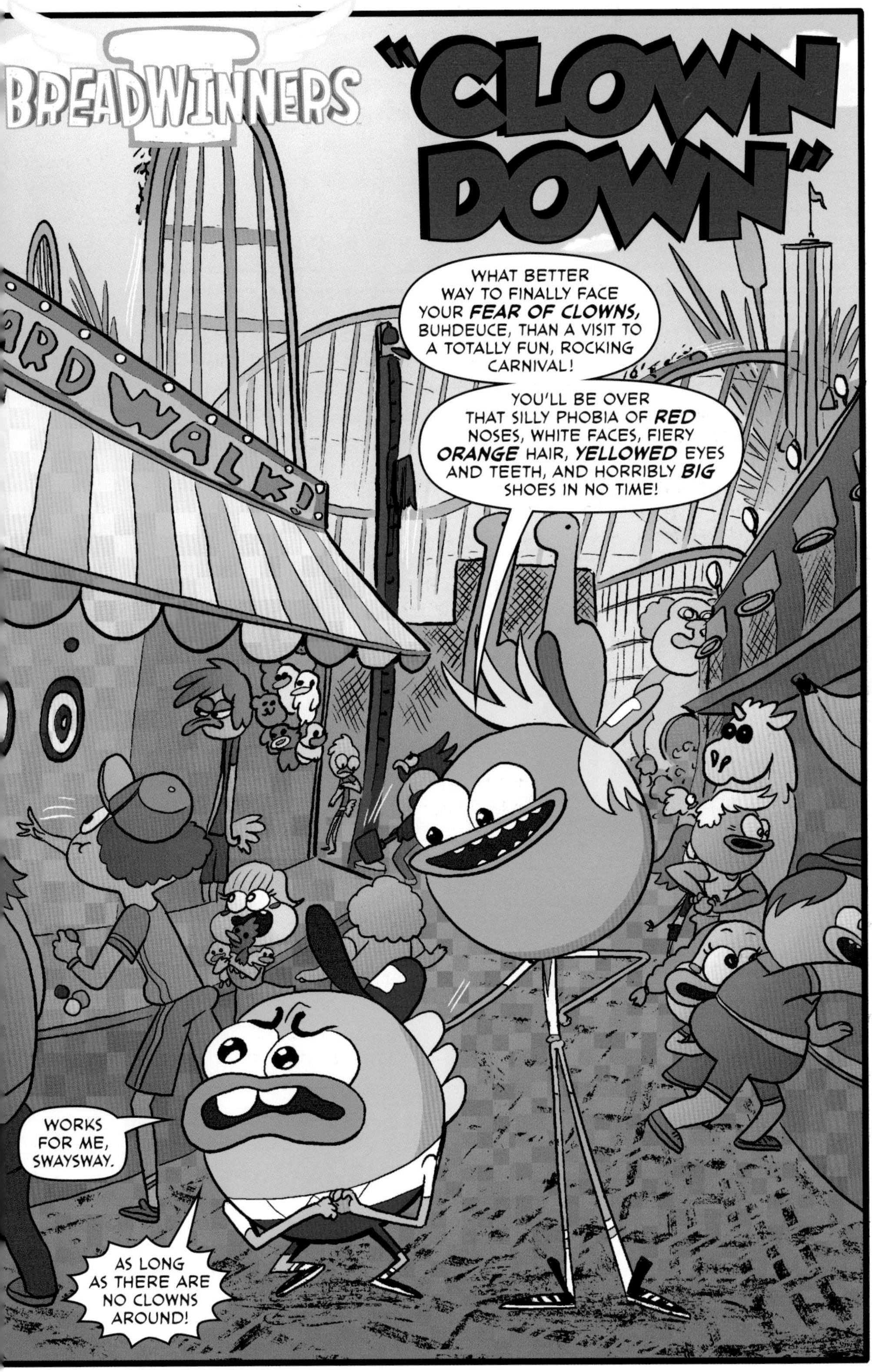
BREADWINNERS
"CLOWN DOWN"
ARDWALK!
WHAT BETTER WAY TO FINALLY FACE YOUR FEAR OF CLOWNS, BUHDEUCE, THAN A VISIT TO A TOTALLY FUN, ROCKING CARNIVAL!
YOU'LL BE OVER THAT SILLY PHOBIA OF RED NOSES, WHITE FACES, FIERY ORANGE HAIR, YELLOWED EYES AND TEETH, AND HORRIBLY BIG SHOES IN NO TIME!
WORKS FOR ME, SWAYSWAY.
AS LONG AS THERE ARE NO CLOWNS AROUND!

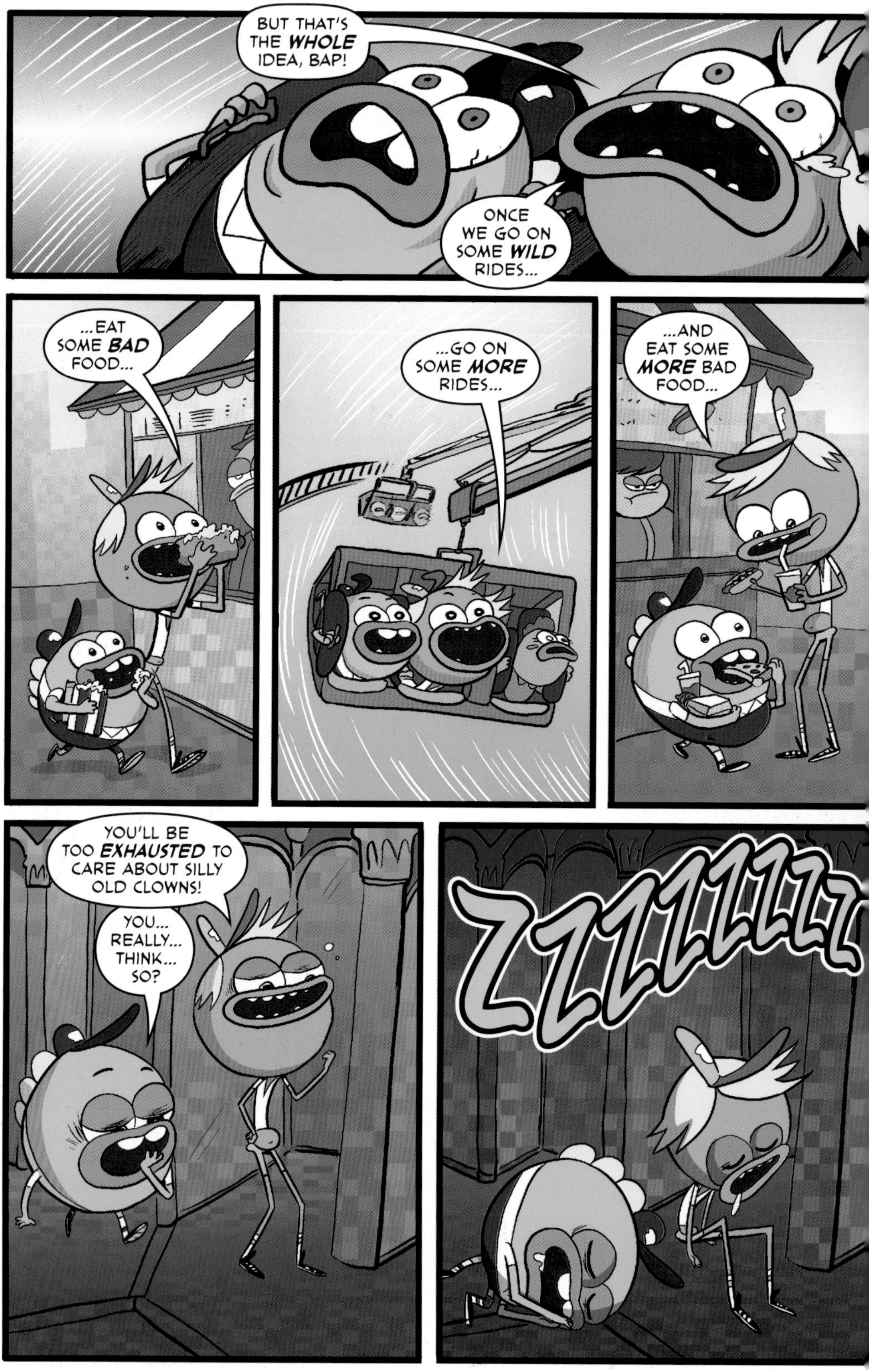
BUT THAT'S THE *WHOLE* IDEA, BAP!
ONCE WE GO ON SOME *WILD* RIDES...
...EAT SOME *BAD* FOOD...
...GO ON SOME *MORE* RIDES...
...AND EAT SOME *MORE* BAD FOOD...
YOU'LL BE TOO *EXHAUSTED* TO CARE ABOUT SILLY OLD CLOWNS!
YOU... REALLY... THINK... SO?
ZZZZZZZZ

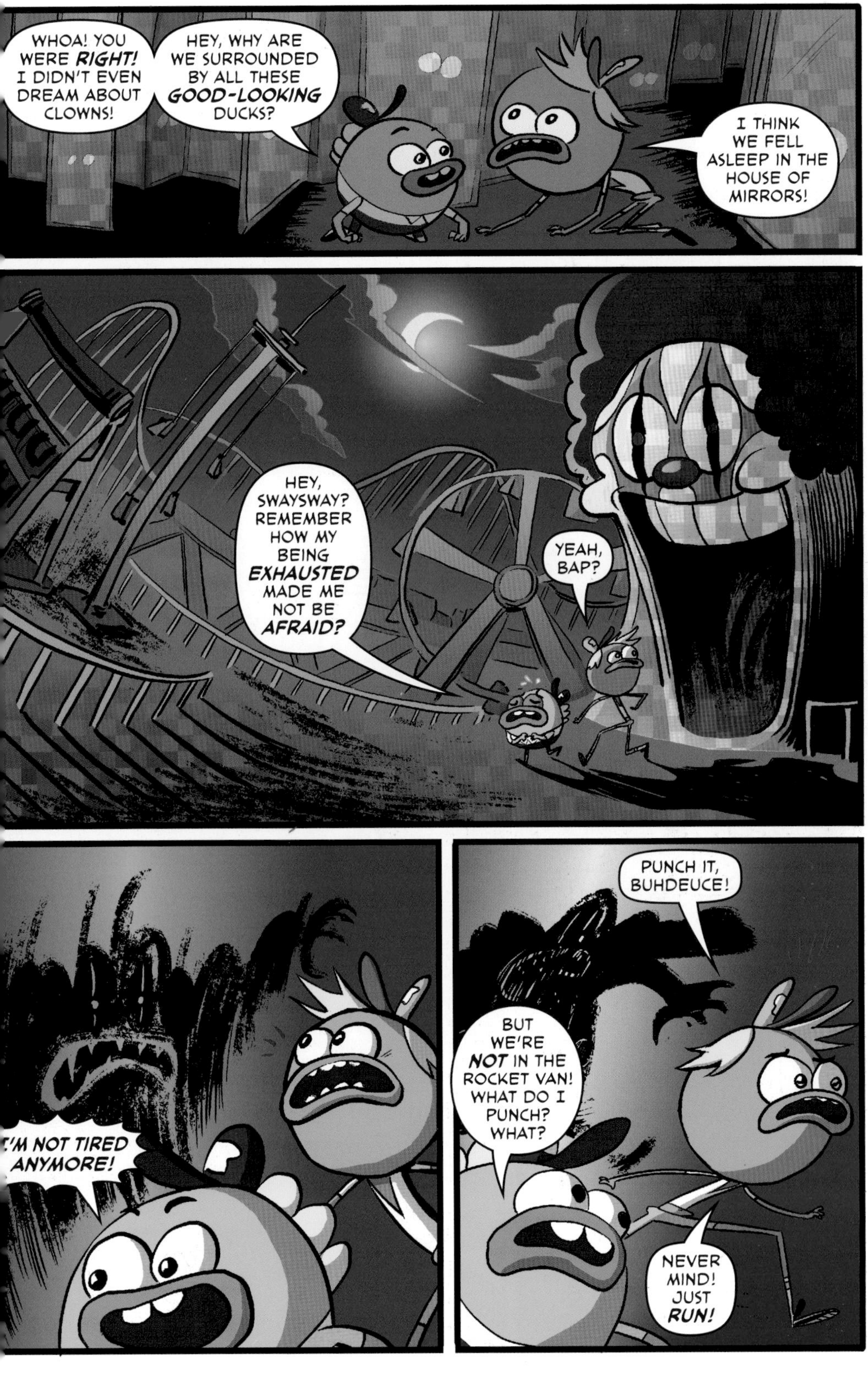
WHOA! YOU WERE RIGHT! I DIDN'T EVEN DREAM ABOUT CLOWNS!
HEY, WHY ARE WE SURROUNDED BY ALL THESE GOOD-LOOKING DUCKS?
I THINK WE FELL ASLEEP IN THE HOUSE OF MIRRORS!
HEY, SWAYSWAY? REMEMBER HOW MY BEING EXHAUSTED MADE ME NOT BE AFRAID?
YEAH, BAP?
I'M NOT TIRED ANYMORE!
PUNCH IT, BUHDEUCE!
BUT WE'RE NOT IN THE ROCKET VAN! WHAT DO I PUNCH? WHAT?
NEVER MIND! JUST RUN!

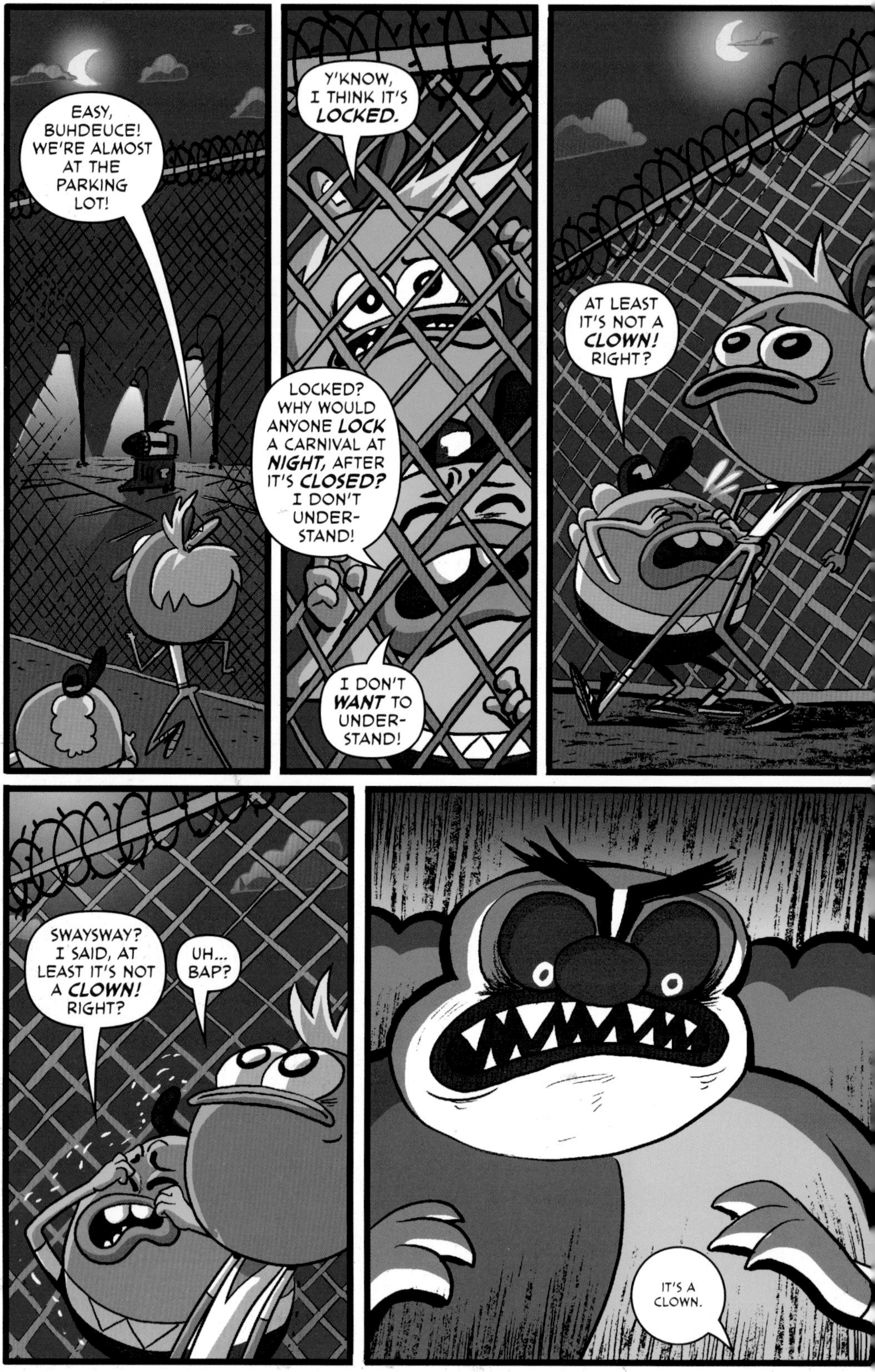
EASY, BUHDEUCE! WE'RE ALMOST AT THE PARKING LOT!
Y'KNOW, I THINK IT'S LOCKED.
LOCKED? WHY WOULD ANYONE LOCK A CARNIVAL AT NIGHT, AFTER IT'S CLOSED? I DON'T UNDER-STAND!
I DON'T WANT TO UNDER-STAND!
AT LEAST IT'S NOT A CLOWN! RIGHT?
SWAYSWAY? I SAID, AT LEAST IT'S NOT A CLOWN! RIGHT?
UH... BAP?
IT'S A CLOWN.

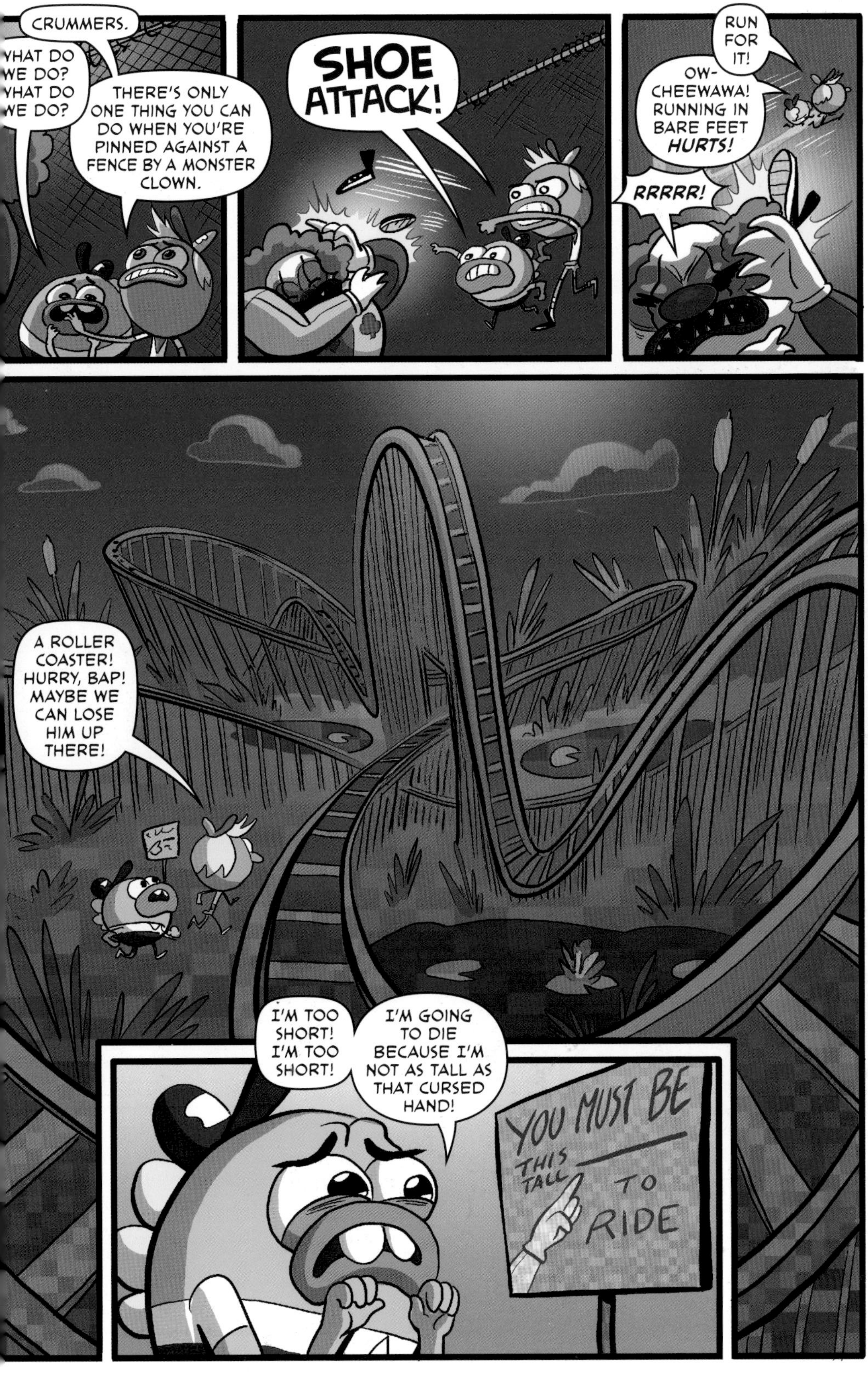
CRUMMERS.
WHAT DO WE DO? WHAT DO WE DO?
THERE'S ONLY ONE THING YOU CAN DO WHEN YOU'RE PINNED AGAINST A FENCE BY A MONSTER CLOWN.
SHOE ATTACK!
RUN FOR IT!
OW-CHEEWAWA! RUNNING IN BARE FEET HURTS!
RRRRR!
A ROLLER COASTER! HURRY, BAP! MAYBE WE CAN LOSE HIM UP THERE!
I'M TOO SHORT! I'M TOO SHORT!
I'M GOING TO DIE BECAUSE I'M NOT AS TALL AS THAT CURSED HAND!
YOU MUST BE THIS TALL TO RIDE

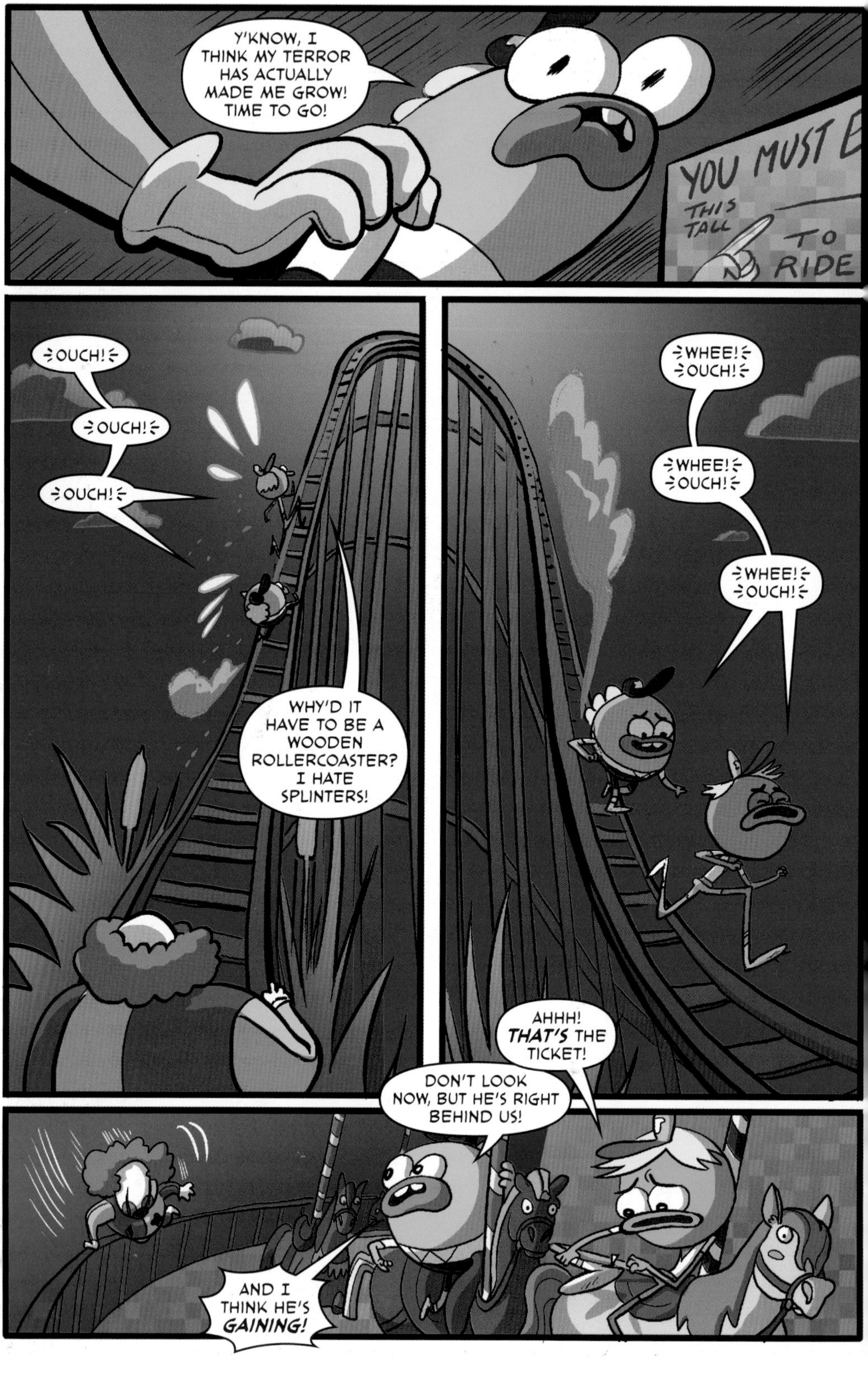
Y'KNOW, I THINK MY TERROR HAS ACTUALLY MADE ME GROW! TIME TO GO!
YOU MUST BE THIS TALL TO RIDE
OUCH!
OUCH!
OUCH!
WHY'D IT HAVE TO BE A WOODEN ROLLERCOASTER? I HATE SPLINTERS!
WHEE! OUCH!
WHEE! OUCH!
WHEE! OUCH!
AHHH! *THAT'S* THE TICKET!
DON'T LOOK NOW, BUT HE'S RIGHT BEHIND US!
AND I THINK HE'S *GAINING!*

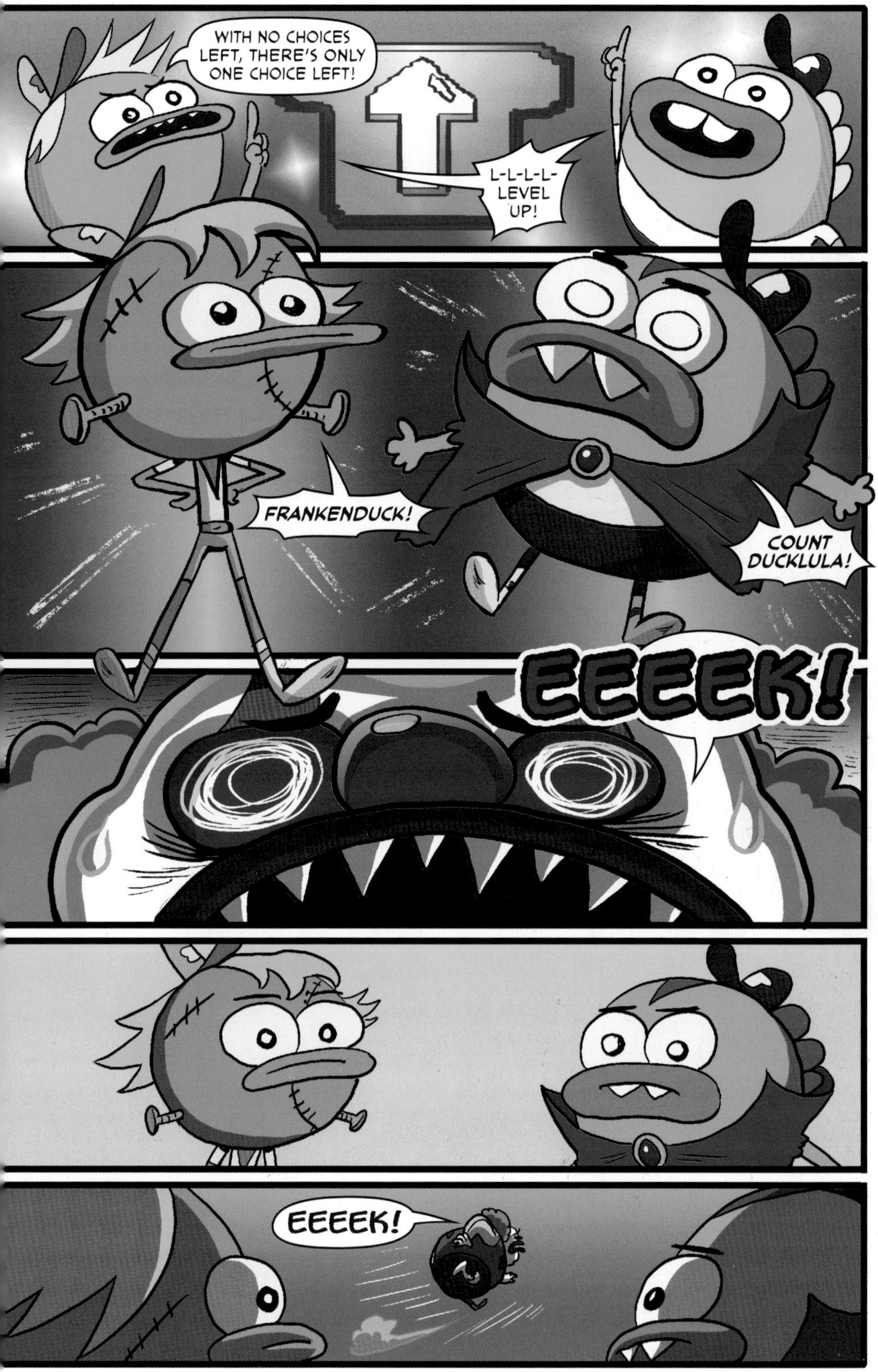
WITH NO CHOICES LEFT, THERE'S ONLY ONE CHOICE LEFT!
L-L-L-L-LEVEL UP!
FRANKENDUCK!
COUNT DUCKLULA!
EEEEK!
EEEEK!

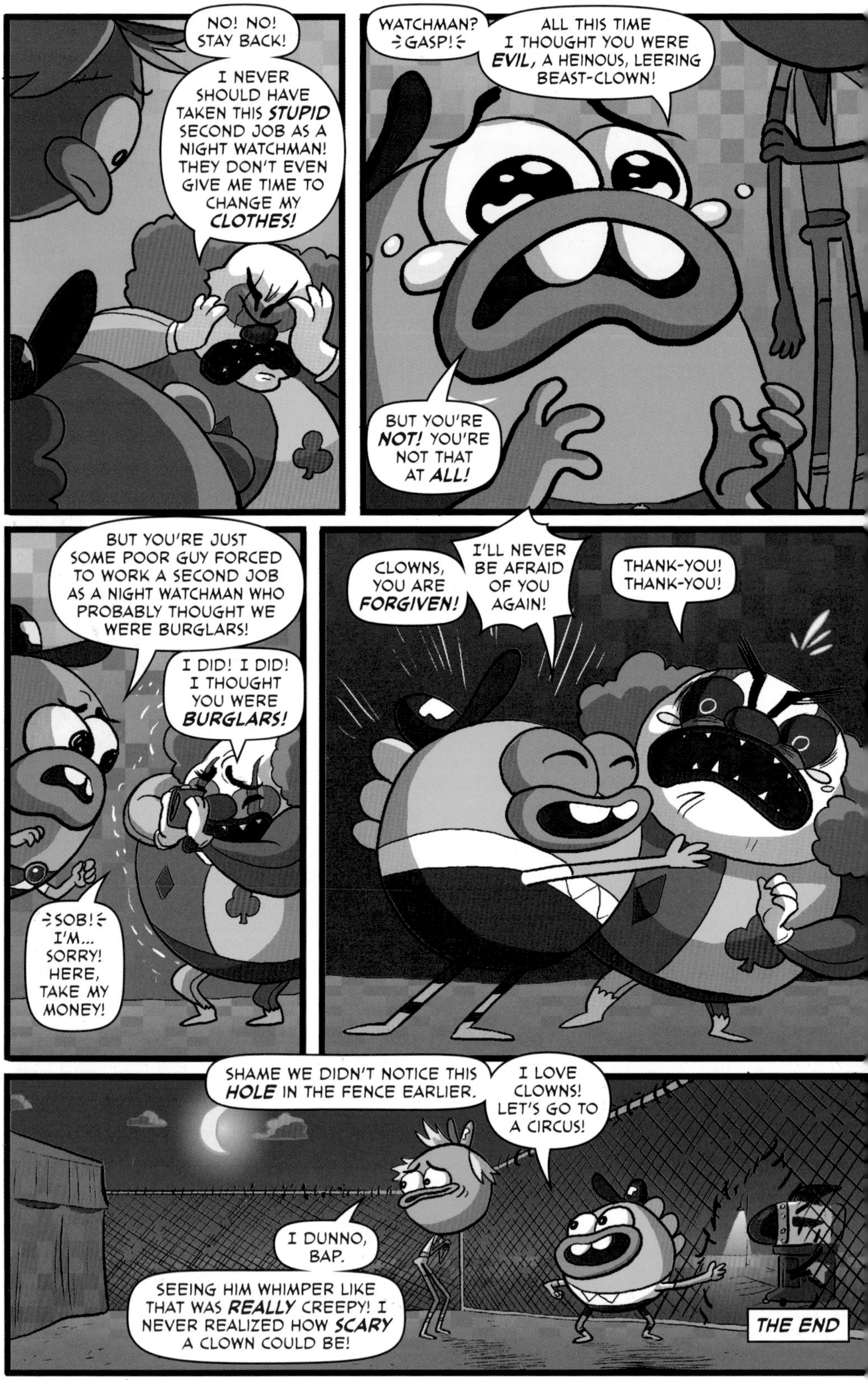

NO! NO! STAY BACK!
I NEVER SHOULD HAVE TAKEN THIS STUPID SECOND JOB AS A NIGHT WATCHMAN! THEY DON'T EVEN GIVE ME TIME TO CHANGE MY CLOTHES!
WATCHMAN? ⁼GASP!⁼
ALL THIS TIME I THOUGHT YOU WERE EVIL, A HEINOUS, LEERING BEAST-CLOWN!
BUT YOU'RE NOT! YOU'RE NOT THAT AT ALL!
BUT YOU'RE JUST SOME POOR GUY FORCED TO WORK A SECOND JOB AS A NIGHT WATCHMAN WHO PROBABLY THOUGHT WE WERE BURGLARS!
I DID! I DID! I THOUGHT YOU WERE BURGLARS!
⁼SOB!⁼ I'M... SORRY! HERE, TAKE MY MONEY!
CLOWNS, YOU ARE FORGIVEN!
I'LL NEVER BE AFRAID OF YOU AGAIN!
THANK-YOU! THANK-YOU!
SHAME WE DIDN'T NOTICE THIS HOLE IN THE FENCE EARLIER.
I LOVE CLOWNS! LET'S GO TO A CIRCUS!
I DUNNO, BAP.
SEEING HIM WHIMPER LIKE THAT WAS REALLY CREEPY! I NEVER REALIZED HOW SCARY A CLOWN COULD BE!
THE END

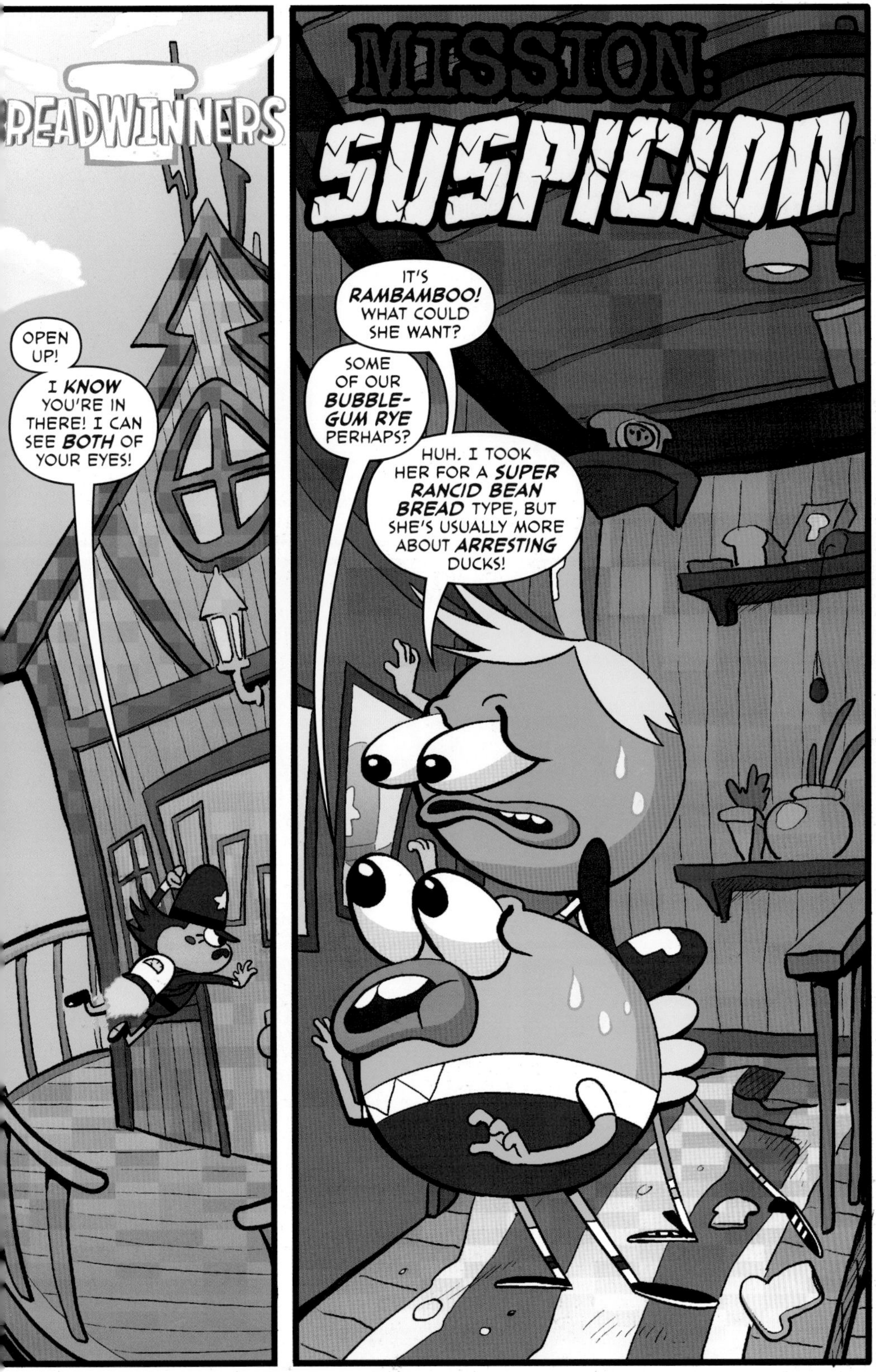
BREADWINNERS
OPEN UP!
I KNOW YOU'RE IN THERE! I CAN SEE BOTH OF YOUR EYES!
MISSION: SUSPICION
IT'S RAMBAMBOO! WHAT COULD SHE WANT?
SOME OF OUR BUBBLE-GUM RYE PERHAPS?
HUH. I TOOK HER FOR A SUPER RANCID BEAN BREAD TYPE, BUT SHE'S USUALLY MORE ABOUT ARRESTING DUCKS!

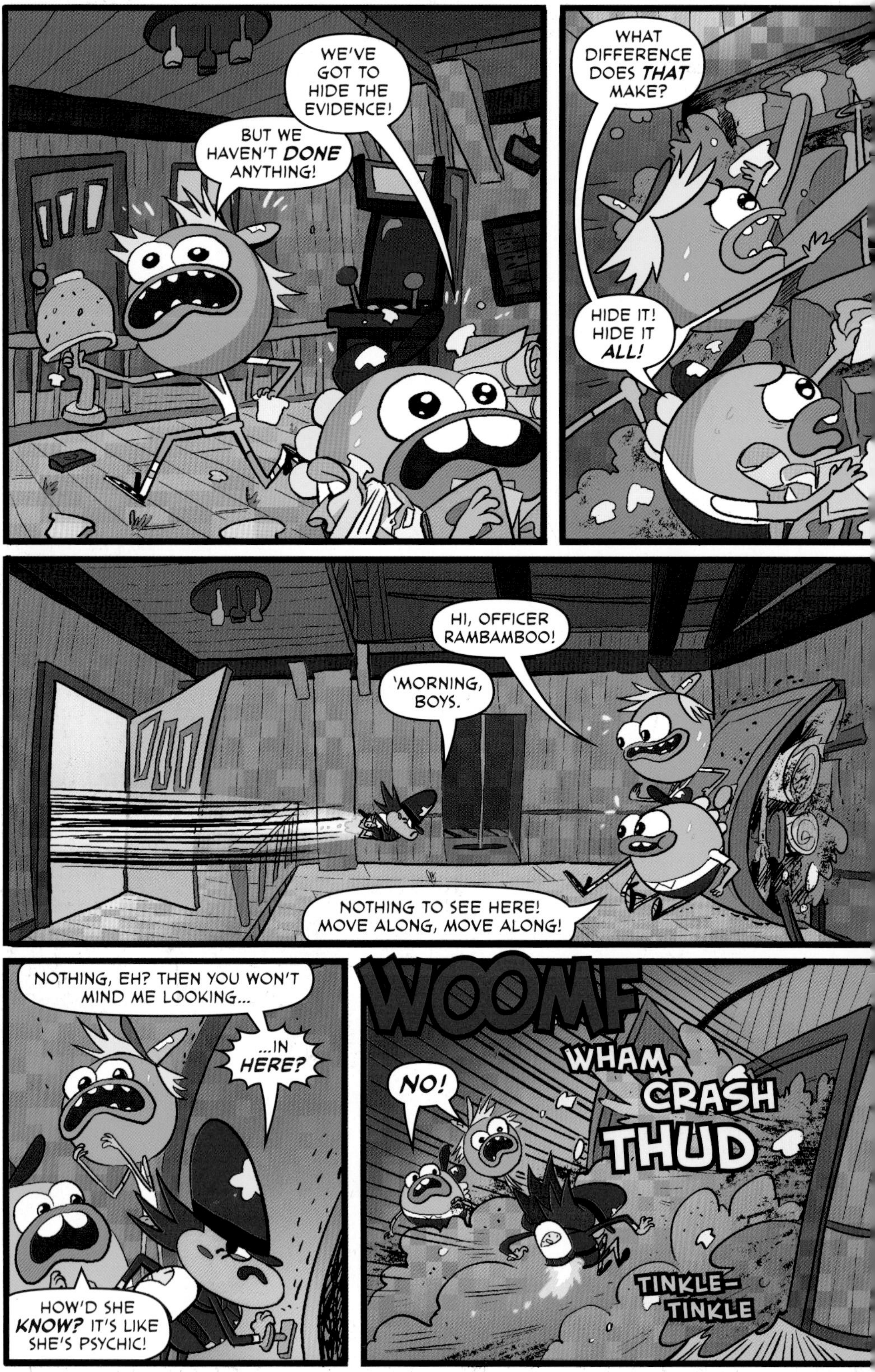
BUT WE HAVEN'T DONE ANYTHING!
WE'VE GOT TO HIDE THE EVIDENCE!
WHAT DIFFERENCE DOES THAT MAKE?
HIDE IT! HIDE IT ALL!
HI, OFFICER RAMBAMBOO!
'MORNING, BOYS.
NOTHING TO SEE HERE! MOVE ALONG, MOVE ALONG!
NOTHING, EH? THEN YOU WON'T MIND ME LOOKING...
...IN HERE?
HOW'D SHE KNOW? IT'S LIKE SHE'S PSYCHIC!
WOOMF
NO!
WHAM
CRASH
THUD
TINKLE-TINKLE

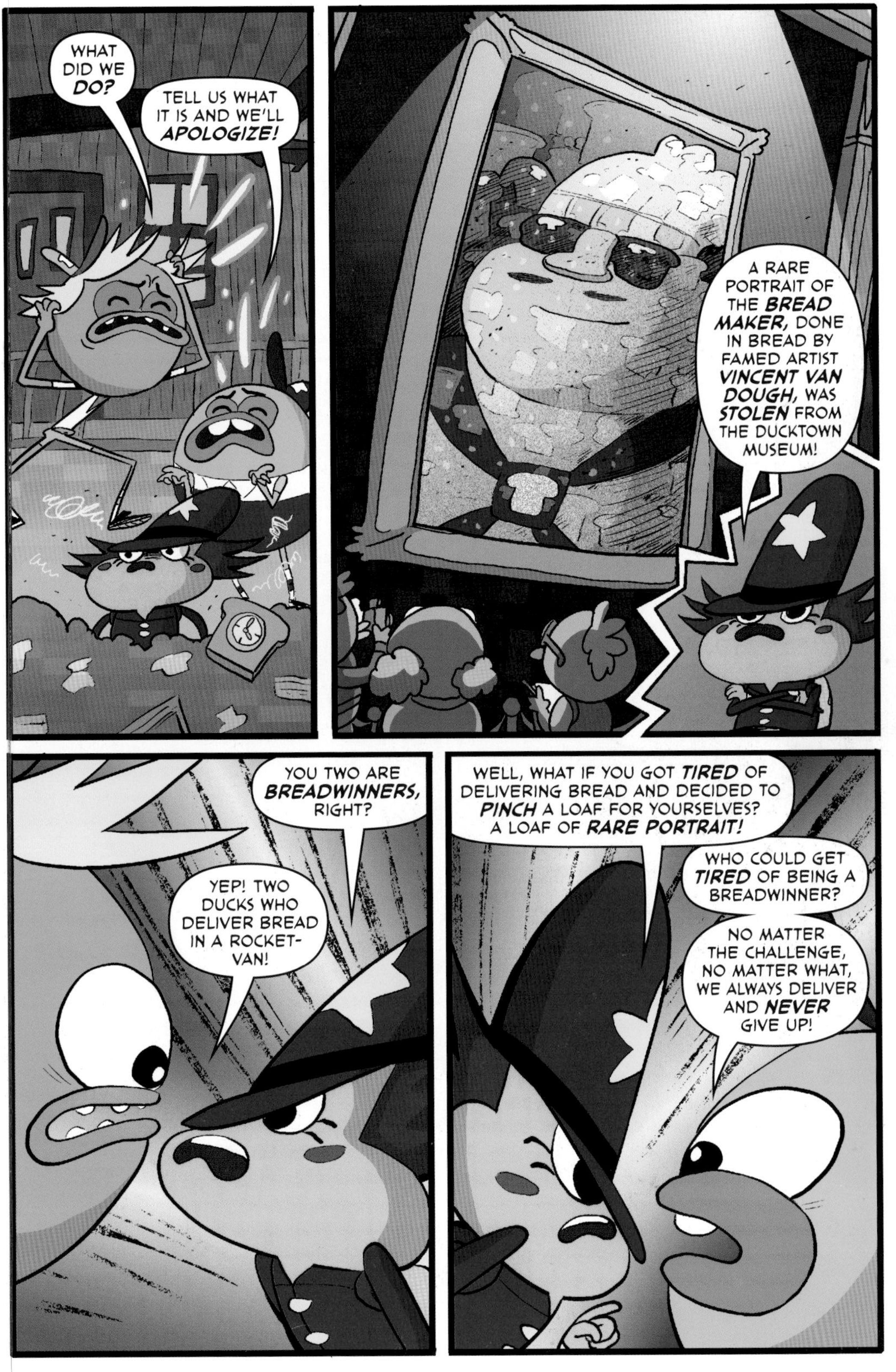
WHAT DID WE *DO?*
TELL US WHAT IT IS AND WE'LL *APOLOGIZE!*
A RARE PORTRAIT OF THE *BREAD MAKER,* DONE IN BREAD BY FAMED ARTIST *VINCENT VAN DOUGH,* WAS *STOLEN* FROM THE DUCKTOWN MUSEUM!
YOU TWO ARE *BREADWINNERS,* RIGHT?
YEP! TWO DUCKS WHO DELIVER BREAD IN A ROCKET-VAN!
WELL, WHAT IF YOU GOT *TIRED* OF DELIVERING BREAD AND DECIDED TO *PINCH* A LOAF FOR YOURSELVES? A LOAF OF *RARE PORTRAIT!*
WHO COULD GET *TIRED* OF BEING A BREADWINNER?
NO MATTER THE CHALLENGE, NO MATTER WHAT, WE ALWAYS DELIVER AND *NEVER* GIVE UP!

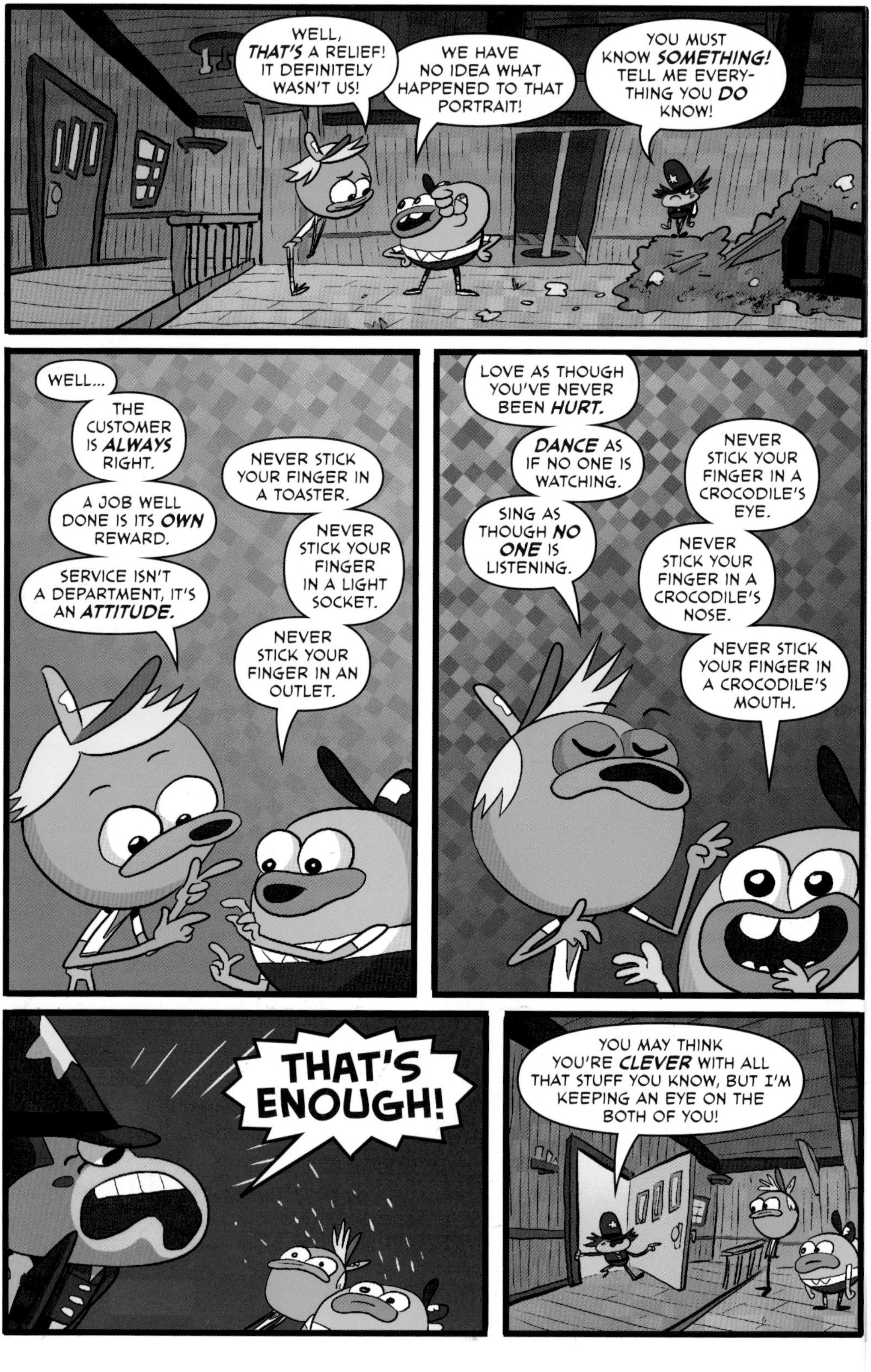
WELL, THAT'S A RELIEF! IT DEFINITELY WASN'T US!
WE HAVE NO IDEA WHAT HAPPENED TO THAT PORTRAIT!
YOU MUST KNOW SOMETHING! TELL ME EVERYTHING YOU DO KNOW!
WELL...
THE CUSTOMER IS ALWAYS RIGHT.
A JOB WELL DONE IS ITS OWN REWARD.
SERVICE ISN'T A DEPARTMENT, IT'S AN ATTITUDE.
NEVER STICK YOUR FINGER IN A TOASTER.
NEVER STICK YOUR FINGER IN A LIGHT SOCKET.
NEVER STICK YOUR FINGER IN AN OUTLET.
LOVE AS THOUGH YOU'VE NEVER BEEN HURT.
DANCE AS IF NO ONE IS WATCHING.
SING AS THOUGH NO ONE IS LISTENING.
NEVER STICK YOUR FINGER IN A CROCODILE'S EYE.
NEVER STICK YOUR FINGER IN A CROCODILE'S NOSE.
NEVER STICK YOUR FINGER IN A CROCODILE'S MOUTH.
THAT'S ENOUGH!
YOU MAY THINK YOU'RE CLEVER WITH ALL THAT STUFF YOU KNOW, BUT I'M KEEPING AN EYE ON THE BOTH OF YOU!

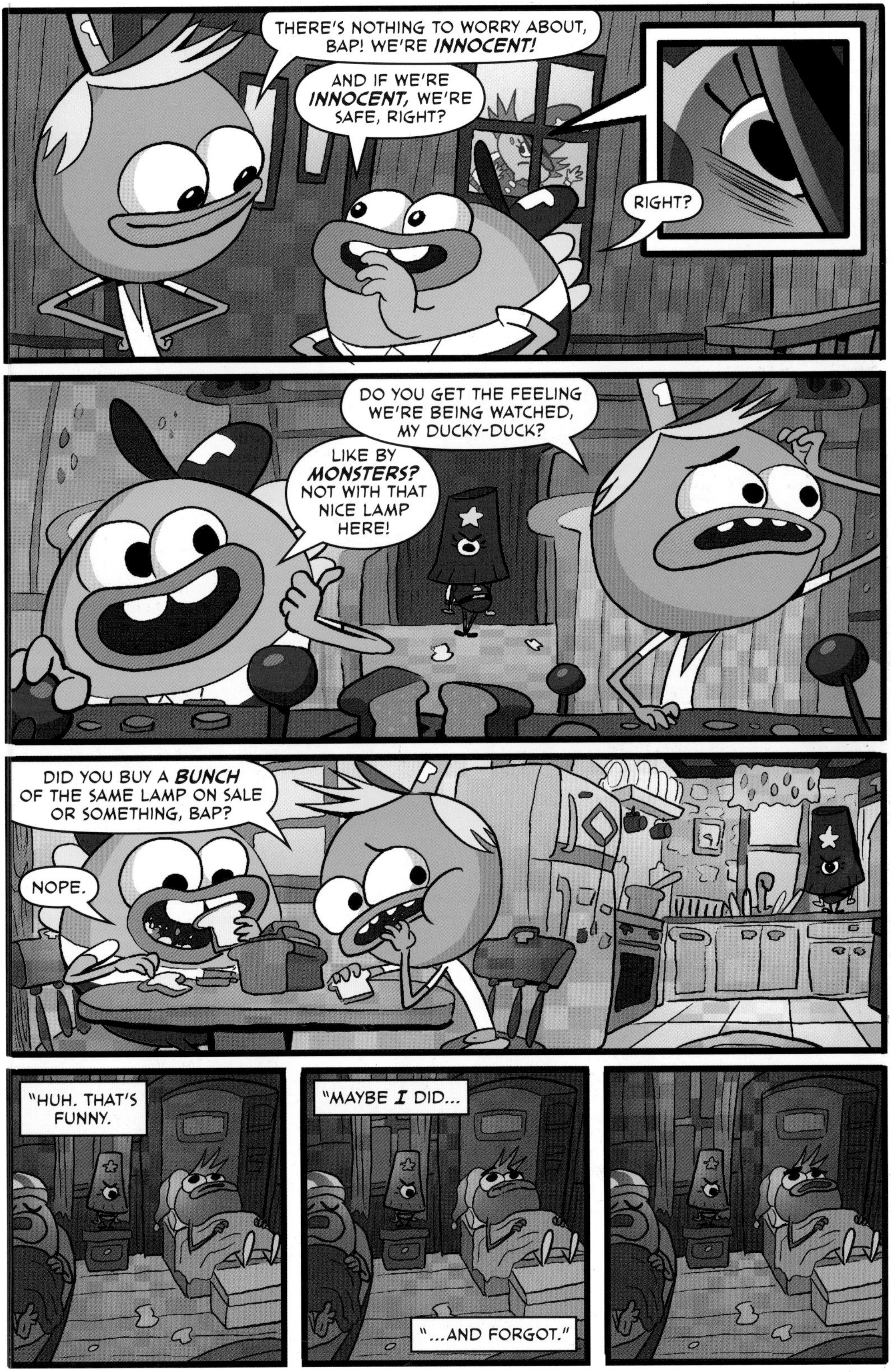
THERE'S NOTHING TO WORRY ABOUT, BAP! WE'RE INNOCENT!
AND IF WE'RE INNOCENT, WE'RE SAFE, RIGHT?
RIGHT?
DO YOU GET THE FEELING WE'RE BEING WATCHED, MY DUCKY-DUCK?
LIKE BY MONSTERS? NOT WITH THAT NICE LAMP HERE!
DID YOU BUY A BUNCH OF THE SAME LAMP ON SALE OR SOMETHING, BAP?
NOPE.
"HUH. THAT'S FUNNY.
"MAYBE I DID...
"...AND FORGOT."

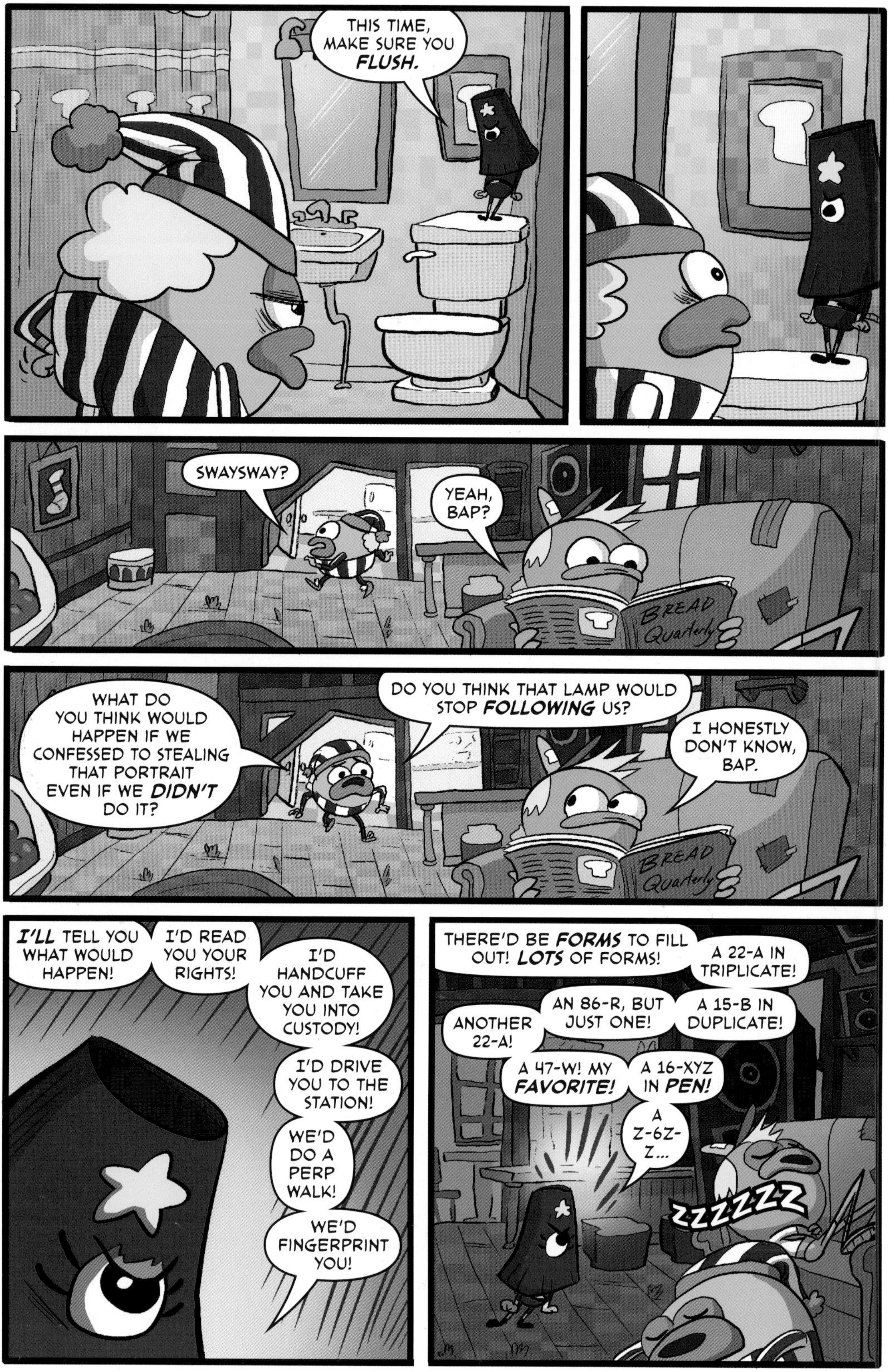
THIS TIME, MAKE SURE YOU FLUSH.
SWAYSWAY?
YEAH, BAP?
BREAD Quarterly
WHAT DO YOU THINK WOULD HAPPEN IF WE CONFESSED TO STEALING THAT PORTRAIT EVEN IF WE DIDN'T DO IT?
DO YOU THINK THAT LAMP WOULD STOP FOLLOWING US?
I HONESTLY DON'T KNOW, BAP.
BREAD Quarterly
I'LL TELL YOU WHAT WOULD HAPPEN!
I'D READ YOU YOUR RIGHTS!
I'D HANDCUFF YOU AND TAKE YOU INTO CUSTODY!
I'D DRIVE YOU TO THE STATION!
WE'D DO A PERP WALK!
WE'D FINGERPRINT YOU!
THERE'D BE FORMS TO FILL OUT! LOTS OF FORMS!
A 22-A IN TRIPLICATE!
AN 86-R, BUT JUST ONE!
A 15-B IN DUPLICATE!
ANOTHER 22-A!
A 47-W! MY FAVORITE!
A 16-XYZ IN PEN!
A Z-6Z-Z...
ZZZZZZ

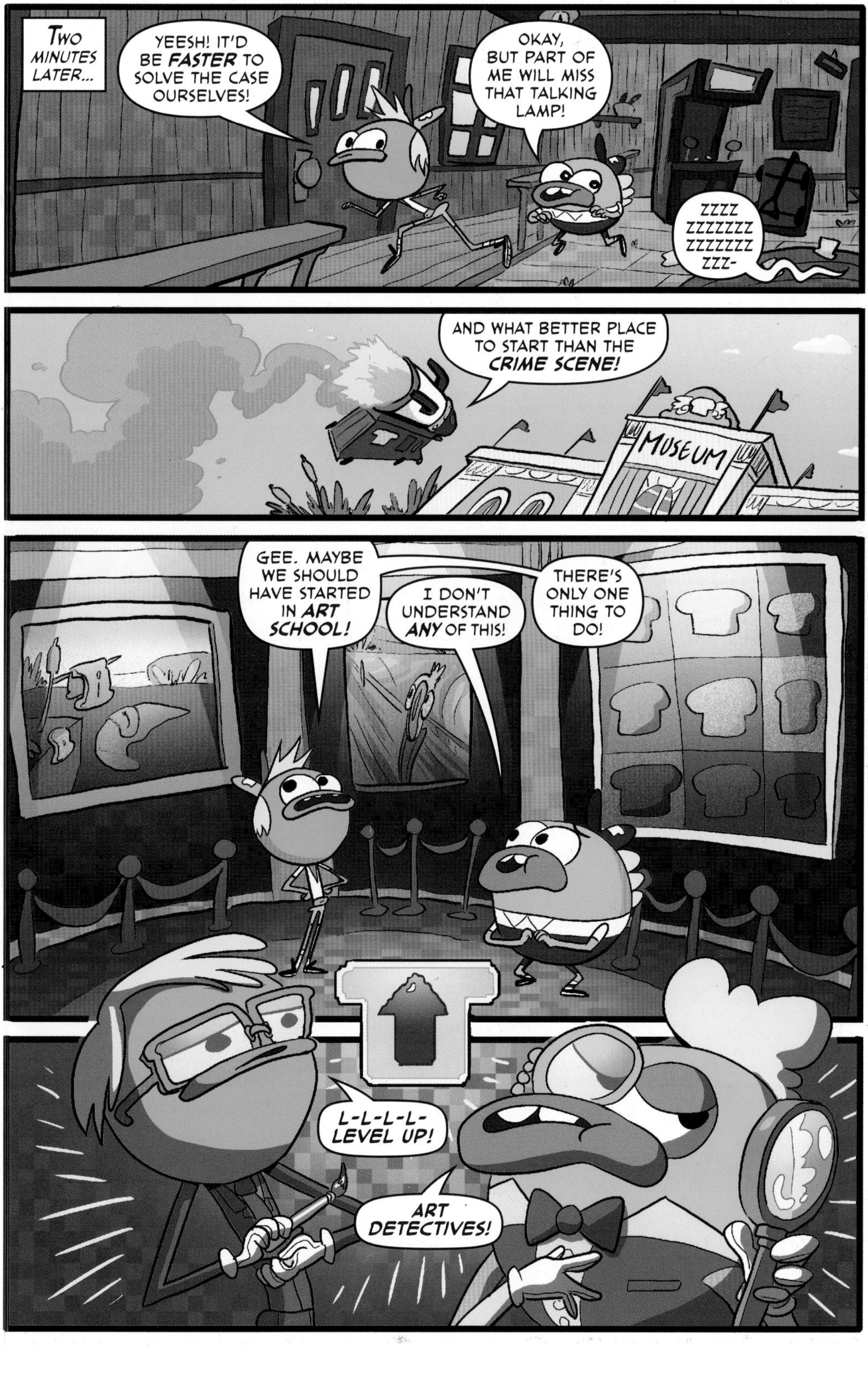
TWO MINUTES LATER...
YEESH! IT'D BE FASTER TO SOLVE THE CASE OURSELVES!
OKAY, BUT PART OF ME WILL MISS THAT TALKING LAMP!
ZZZZ ZZZZZZZ ZZZZZZZ ZZZ-
AND WHAT BETTER PLACE TO START THAN THE CRIME SCENE!
MUSEUM
GEE. MAYBE WE SHOULD HAVE STARTED IN ART SCHOOL!
I DON'T UNDERSTAND ANY OF THIS!
THERE'S ONLY ONE THING TO DO!
L-L-L-L-LEVEL UP!
ART DETECTIVES!

THE *WISSY-WOO* OF THE WACKY-WOO MAKES THE DEVIOUS SIMPLICITY OF THE *BLAH-BLAH-BLAH* REMARKABLE!

YET THE *MEKKA LEKKA HI MEKKA HINEY HO* CLEARLY UNDERMINES THE *SCOTTY-WADDY-DOO-DOO* OF THE SUBSTRUCTURE!

SAY, THIS PAINTING'S KINDA.... *DRIPPING...*

≍YAWN≍

ART ISN'T *BORING!* IT'S YOUR *FRIEND!*

COME PLAY WITH US, BUHDEUCE! WE'LL TELL YOU WHAT YOU NEED TO KNOW!

THAT WHICH YOU SEEK ISN'T *LOST!*

FOR YOU *CANNOT* LOSE WHAT NEVER LEFT!

LOST? LEFT? STOP MAKING MY *BRAIN HURT* AND TELL ME WHAT YOU'RE TRYING TO SAY!

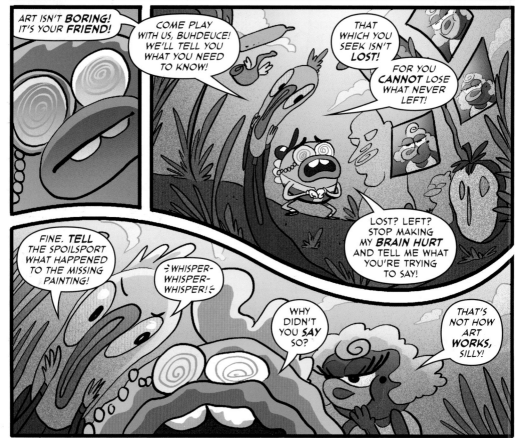

FINE. *TELL* THE SPOILSPORT WHAT HAPPENED TO THE MISSING PAINTING!

≍WHISPER-WHISPER-WHISPER!≍

WHY DIDN'T YOU *SAY* SO?

THAT'S NOT HOW ART *WORKS,* SILLY!

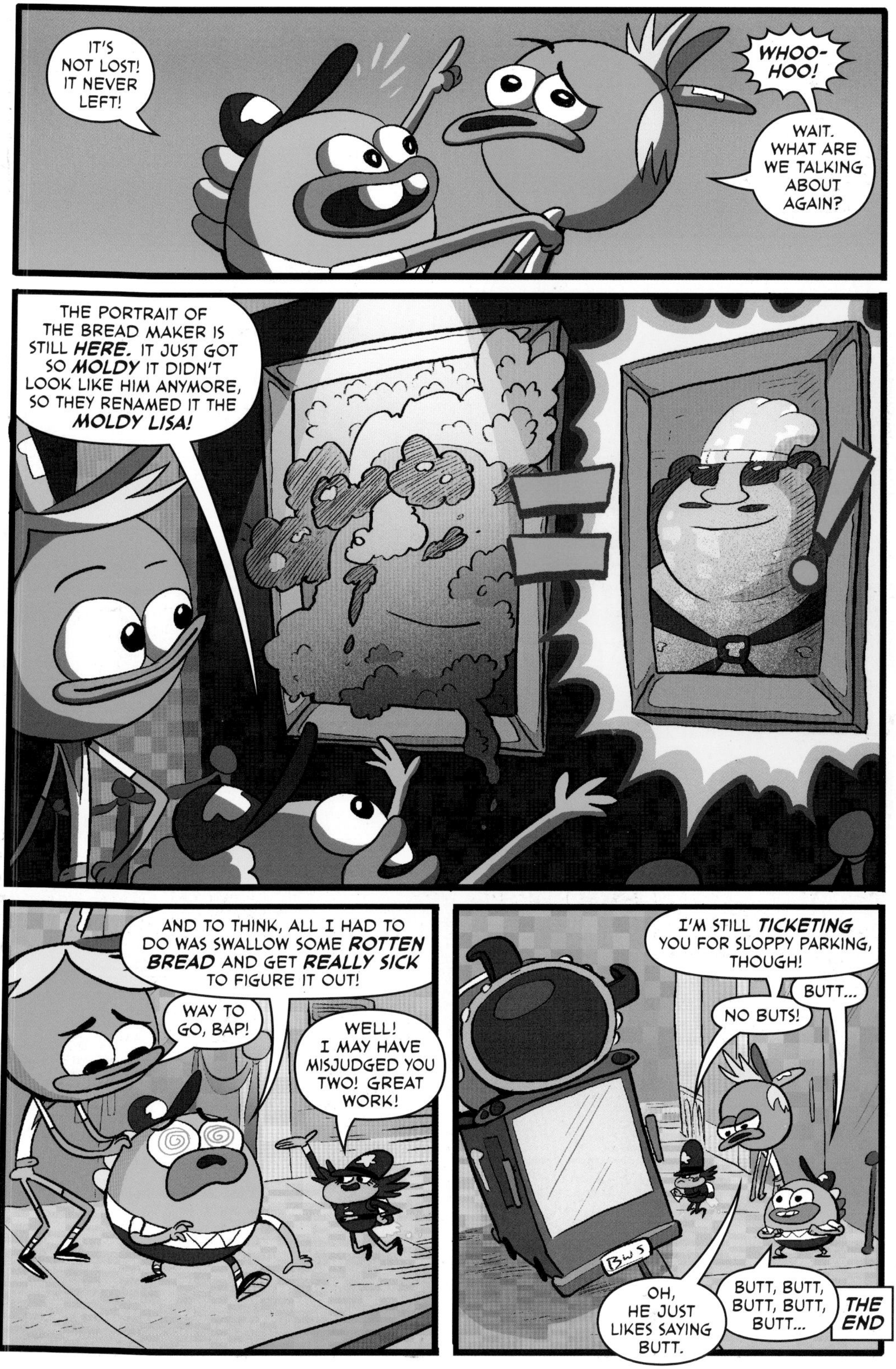
IT'S NOT LOST! IT NEVER LEFT!
WHOO-HOO!
WAIT. WHAT ARE WE TALKING ABOUT AGAIN?
THE PORTRAIT OF THE BREAD MAKER IS STILL HERE. IT JUST GOT SO MOLDY IT DIDN'T LOOK LIKE HIM ANYMORE, SO THEY RENAMED IT THE MOLDY LISA!
AND TO THINK, ALL I HAD TO DO WAS SWALLOW SOME ROTTEN BREAD AND GET REALLY SICK TO FIGURE IT OUT!
WAY TO GO, BAP!
WELL! I MAY HAVE MISJUDGED YOU TWO! GREAT WORK!
I'M STILL TICKETING YOU FOR SLOPPY PARKING, THOUGH!
BUTT...
NO BUTS!
OH, HE JUST LIKES SAYING BUTT.
BUTT, BUTT, BUTT, BUTT, BUTT...
THE END

nickelodeon ™
GRAPHIC NOVELS ARE HERE

ONLY FROM PAPERCUT Z

ON SALE NOW!

ON SALE NOW!

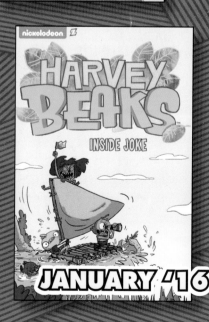

JANUARY '16

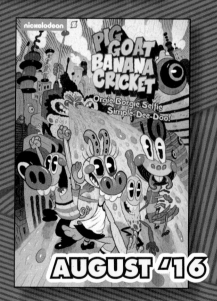

AUGUST '16

WATCH ALL THESE ANIMATED SERIES ON NICKELODEON!